GATHER BY THE GHOST LIGHT: YEAR FOUR

Edited by

JONATHAN COOK

DEDICATION

Family. Friends. Fellow playwrights. Fellow Actors. And everyone who has had faith in me and supported my creative endeavors through the years. You are always there. Cheering me on. I see you and I thank you.

DEDICATION

Family. Friends. Fellow playwrights. Fellow Actors. And everyone who has had faith in me and supported my creative endeavors through the years. You are always there. Cheering me on. I see you and I thank you.

CONTENTS

FOREWORD

<u>TITLE MUSIC CUE:</u>
<u>"9th CRANIAL NERVE"</u>
<u>by JK/47</u>

Greetings! Good day! And welcome back to Gather by the Ghost Light[1]. YEAR FOUR! I'm Jonathan Cook. Your host, producer, and sometimes voice actor on this thing. What a crazy journey this has been and our fourth year has been one of the most pivotal moments for Gather by the Ghost Light. Producing short plays has always been our normal routine, but this was the first year we released two full-length audio plays, which one of those was a live event recorded in front of a sold-out audience! Our first LIVE event and it was a success thanks to our many supporters like you!

Two other major things happened during year four. We were incorporated into a nonprofit organization, and we were also invited to onboard with the Broadway Podcast Network[2]. We are grateful for the opportunities we've been given and these two huge steps have helped us grow tremendously. Ultimately, this was a year of discovery for not only us but also for our audience as more people were discovering us than ever! As I say every year, it's all just further proof that theatre is alive and well in all forms.

One last major step forward we took in our fourth year was launching our own script publishing division called Ghost Light Publications[3]. While we are known for producing our stellar immersive audio plays, there are many full-length scripts for the stage that we love but don't have the bandwidth to fit into our season. But now we have an avenue to get those plays out to a wider audience for our writers and we also have things in motion to start staging full-length works regularly at our local theatre in Augusta, GA.

So, here it is. I present to you another companion book. If you're familiar with our previous annual anthologies, then you know the deal. If not, here's the pitch. What you'll find in the following pages are the full audio play scripts for each episode released during the fourth year of the podcast along with a foreword from each playwright giving you a little extra behind the scenes insight to their

i

play (and fair warning, but some of the commentary before the scripts may include spoilers, so if you've never heard the audio play and you're reading the script for the first time, save the playwright commentary for after). Also included is the original production information for each play showing when and where it first premiered on stage (as the majority of these scripts were originally written as stage plays). There are two exceptions this time around though. As stated earlier, we produced two full-length plays this season and, unfortunately, you won't find the scripts for those within this book due to their higher page counts.

My name may be on the cover but consider this book a collective work by many authors. We thank you for reading. We thank you for listening. And we thank you for being a part of this journey as we Gather by the Ghost Light.

So, for your reading pleasure, here are all the short audio scripts from year four of Gather by the Ghost Light. These are the same adapted scripts that the voice actors used during the recording process and include the sound effect and music cue notes. And there's also a free audio book available! Just tune into the podcast and find the titles of each episode! … I know, I know. Same lame joke as previous years, but you either smiled or scoffed for a moment there, so mission accomplished.

I would like to thank the playwrights as well as the voice actors who have contributed to bringing these stories to life and also the Broadway Podcast Network for onboarding us to their platform. I would also like to thank the new and longtime listeners who have been tuning in for every episode. Your support is what gives me the passion and drive to keep this thing going. Also, a huge thank you to my family who have supported all my creative endeavors over the years.

Now, gather around the ghost light. Sit back and enjoy. This is Gather by the Ghost Light: Year Four.

GBTGL creator and executive director: *Jonathan Cook*

Episode 4.1
A MONOGAMY OF SWANS
(Release date: May 23, 2023)

Written by John Minigan

Originally premiered as a stage play as part of the Funky Little Theatre Company's[4] [spectrum]: lgbt festival in Colorado Springs, CO in March 2016. Directed by Luke Schoenemann. Original cast – Haley Hunsaker (Ellie); and Kristen Gutzeit (Violet).

Synopsis: After breaking up with her fiancé Jimmie, Ellie has gone to Boston's Public Garden to kill the swans. Violet, her ex, arrives with a better alternative.

<u>Audio Play Production</u>
Produced and directed by Jonathan Cook.
Cast: Devon McSherry (Ellie); and Shelby Lauren Smith (Violet).
Music cue(s): "A Soaring Swan Sister" by Ardie Son.

Author (John Minigan) Commentary: I grew up in Massachusetts and spent a long time refusing to include the voices that I heard growing up in my plays. I foolishly thought they weren't characters to put in a "real play." A Monogamy of Swans is the first time I really leaned into those voices and those characters, wanting to find their warmth, their humor, and their compassion.

By the way, the two swans on the lagoon in Boston's Public Garden are, in fact, named Romeo and Juliet. And, yes, they are both female.

For licensing rights to this play, contact the playwright directly at john.a.minigan@gmail.com.

<u>SCRIPT: A MONOGAMY OF SWANS</u>

<u>CHARACTERS</u>

ELLIE...   A Bostonian, early-mid 20s.

VIOLET...   A former Bostonian, also early-mid 20s.

<u>SETTING</u>

Boston. The Public Garden near the lagoon. A quiet morning in spring.

<u>OPENING MUSIC CUE: "A SOARING SWAN SISTER"</u>

<u>SUMMER AMBIENCE.</u>

<u>SWANS ARE HEARD IN THE DISTANCE.</u>

<u>ELLIE GRUNTS AS SHE IS THROWING PIECES OF BREAD AT THE SWANS.</u>

ELLIE: Come on, you frickin' no-good... Come on! Come on! You little bastards, I'm gonna get you, so help me God. Yeah, you keep your distance, 'you know what's good for you.

<u>FOOTSTEPS AS VIOLET APPROACHES.</u>

VIOLET: (DISTANCE) Ellie?

ELLIE: Oh, shit.

VIOLET: (DISTANCE) Ellie, is that you down here?

ELLIE: No, it's not me!

VIOLET: Ellie!

ELLIE: Aw, for crissake! What are you doing here?

VIOLET: I tried your apartment first. I figured you were probably here.

ELLIE: How you figure I'm at the Public Garden?

VIOLET: 'Cause I saw Facebook. I figured something was, you know. I figured I better drive down and see what you were doing.

ELLIE: You drove all the way down from Haverhill just to see what I was doing?

VIOLET: 'Cause I saw what you put on Facebook. (LOOKING OUT) That's them?

ELLIE: Little bastards.

VIOLET: You shouldn't put on Facebook you're going to kill them. Wha'd you do, poison the bread?

ELLIE: Don't believe everything you see on the internet, all right? I'm just feeding them.

VIOLET: Why you feeding them if you're gonna kill them?

ELLIE: That is so like you, you know? Asking questions.

'Cause you always gotta have your "information." Well, let me tell you something: life is not just a bunch of questions. Because if life was just a bunch of questions, you'd spend all your time asking them and maybe you'd get an answer and maybe the answer you get wouldn't be good for anybody, and you'd realize maybe you should have kept your fat mouth shut.

> ELLIE PICKS UP A ROCK AND PREPARES TO THROW IT.

VIOLET: That is a rock.

ELLIE: I know it's a rock.

VIOLET: Are you gonna throw a rock at the swans?

ELLIE: What, you want me throw it at you?

VIOLET: What have you got against them?

ELLIE: That's another good question. Why don't we ask? (CALLING OUT TO THE SWANS) Hey, frickin' swans! I'm thinking I might throw this rock and it might hit you and Vi here would like an explanation for why I would do that. Do you have an explanation?

> SILENCE.

They got no answer. Filled with secrets. Filled with deception.

VIOLET: I'm sorry about you and

	Jimmie.
ELLIE:	I don't want to talk about Jimmie.
VIOLET:	I'm sorry he left.
ELLIE:	Oh, yeahyeahyeah, you're prob'ly all broken up about that.
VIOLET:	He didn't deserve you.
ELLIE:	Is that why you drove down from Haverhill? Because Jimmie didn't deserve me?
VIOLET:	I drove down 'cause you put on Facebook how you were going to kill the swans. "The best thing I could do this morning would be to go down the Public Garden and kill the frickin' swans." Who writes "frickin'" on Facebook?

    <u>ELLIE GRUNTS AS SHE
STARTS TO THROW THE
ROCK.</u>

Do not throw the rock! It isn't their fault he left. That was an experiment, you going out with Jimmie.

ELLIE:	It was not an experiment.
VIOLET:	It was an experiment: you tried it and it didn't work out. Now, drop the rock.

    <u>ELLIE DROPS THE ROCK.</u>

ELLIE:	There. Happy?

    <u>THEY SIT ON THE GROUND.</u>

Hey, hands to yourself, alright?

VIOLET: I thought maybe you needed a hug. I didn't mean anything.

ELLIE: You were the experiment, Vi. Not Jimmie.

VIOLET: We were together two years, and that's an experiment?

ELLIE: Then we broke up. I was all set up to marry Jimmie.

VIOLET: You tried and it didn't work.

ELLIE: You hear Jimmie left, you drive down from Haverhill because you think maybe all of a sudden I'm gonna be... You know.

VIOLET: I drove down 'cause, you kill these swans, they're gonna lock you up.

ELLIE: I'm feeding them.

            ELLIE STANDS AND TOSSES BREAD.

See?

VIOLET: You definitely didn't poison the bread?

ELLIE: What kind of a person do you think I am?

VIOLET: I don't know, but they're keeping their distance, now. You see what you did?

ELLIE: For the reception, my mother was gonna have us put swans on the wedding cake. You know, instead of man and wife? Two swans, kissing with their necks making that little heart shape. And she wanted this ice sculpture of swans, only with their bodies

	all filled up with, like, honeydew melon.
VIOLET:	That's nice.
ELLIE:	It's not nice. You know how long an ice sculpture's gonna last? You get a swan with a melted neck and a gut full of melon. That's supposed to be romantic? What a stupid woman. A stupid woman with a stupid idea.
VIOLET:	It's because they mate for life.
ELLIE:	That's the other internet thing that is completely wrong.
VIOLET:	What are you talking about?
ELLIE:	Swans mating for life. Not true.
VIOLET:	That's supposed to be, like, a scientific fact.
ELLIE:	Well, the scientists forgot the detail that swans pretty much all look alike. They assumed it was always the same two swans. They screw around like everybody else. Little bastards!

ELLIE ANGRILY THROWS
MORE BREAD.

VIOLET:	Where'd you hear this?
ELLIE:	From Jimmie.
VIOLET:	Was he...? You know—
ELLIE:	His upstairs neighbor.
VIOLET:	Oh, I met that one. I hate her.

ELLIE:	And his downstairs neighbor.
VIOLET:	No.
ELLIE:	Yeah.
VIOLET:	I hate her, too.
ELLIE:	And that one across the street from him, undoes her top when she tans?
VIOLET:	At least, now you know.
ELLIE:	And the countergirl at Dunkin's with the side ponytail?
VIOLET:	Her?
ELLIE:	Her mother.
VIOLET:	Jesus.
ELLIE:	I said, "We're supposed to get married Thanksgiving. We're supposed to have swans on the wedding cake." "Well, Ellie, you may not be aware of this, but swans, contrary to popular blah blah blah." He saw it on the internet.
VIOLET:	That's just what they're like.
ELLIE:	So he says. (SHOUTING AT SWANS) You're lousy frickin' role models!
VIOLET:	I mean men, Ellie. It's what they're like. He was an experiment. You tried.
ELLIE:	Listen, Vi—
VIOLET:	Where's Jimmie right now? He must have seen Facebook, right? He knew what you were gonna do and where is he? Did he come down here to make

	sure you didn't do something terrible?
ELLIE:	I would'a thrown the rock at him.
VIOLET:	He would'a deserved it. Come here. Sit down.

<u>THEY BOTH SIT.</u>

	You said you thought we shouldn't be together. You met this guy Jimmie and you thought maybe things were gonna be different. It didn't work out.
ELLIE:	Why'd you let me try?
VIOLET"	'Cause I know about us. I know how I feel about you. I figured, you go ahead, try being with a guy, but it's not going to last 'cause I know how you feel about me.
ELLIE:	I don't think you and me—
VIOLET:	(INTERRUPTING) These swans? I looked them up. They're called Romeo and Juliet.
ELLIE:	You looked on the internet?
VIOLET:	This one's true.
ELLIE:	Well, Juliet's lucky there's just the two of them, 'cause Romeo would be flapping around with all the others.
VIOLET:	They're both girls.
ELLIE:	What are you talking about?
VIOLET:	Seriously. Two girl swans. They've been together, like, ten years.
ELLIE:	How do they know this? Swans

	pretty much all look alike.
VIOLET:	They're the same pair.
ELLIE:	No kidding. Massachusetts, right?
VIOLET:	I don't know about mating for life. But ten years. I figure that's pretty good for swans. They know how they feel about each other.
ELLIE:	I guess they do.
VIOLET:	Hey. Gimme some of the bread.
ELLIE:	I scared them off, they're not gonna—
VIOLET:	Just gimme some.

<u>MUSIC CUE:</u>
<u>"A SOARING SWAN SISTER"</u>

	(CALLING OUT TO THE SWANS WHILE MAKING KISSY NOISES) Swans! Come here! Swanny Swan! Come here! Want some bread?
ELLIE:	You're telling me you drove down all the way from Haverhill just so I wouldn't do something stupid?
VIOLET:	Yeah, I did. Look, look, look. They're coming in. My turn to feed 'em.
ELLIE:	Maybe you better not give 'em that bread.
VIOLET:	Why not? (PAUSE) No, you didn't really... (WHISPERS) poison the bread, did you?
ELLIE:	(LAUGHING) Of course I didn't.
VIOLET:	I should hope not. Here they

	are.
ELLIE:	Hey, look at that.
VIOLET:	Making the little heart shape with their necks.
ELLIE:	I didn't think they really did that.
VIOLET:	I guess they know how they feel about each other.
ELLIE:	I guess they do.

<u>END OF PLAY</u>

Episode 4.2 & 4.3
HUGO SAVES CHRISTMAS…IN MAY
(Release date: May 31, 2023)

Written by Steven Hayet.

"Hugo Saves Christmas… in May!" was commissioned by the Roaring Epiphany Production Company[5] and had its world premiere at Alchemical Studios, located at 50 W17th St. in NYC in May 2023. It was directed by REPC's Co-Artistic Directors, RJ VerChaud and Jillian Faye Liebman. Original cast – Ethan Thomas (Hugo McGee); Lex E. Rojas (Maya Kaplan); Maxine Turenne (Catherine McGee); and Haley Rice (Rachel Kaplan).

Synopsis: A year-round Christmas store is going out of business and Hugo, a longtime loyal customer, refuses to accept the news.

<u>Audio Play Production</u>
Produced and directed by Jonathan Cook.
Cast: Marian Thibodeau (Maya); Adam Cowart (Hugo); Amy Patton (Catherine); and Pepper Wren (Rachel).

Author (Steven Hayet) Commentary: In December 2021, RJ & Jillian approached me about writing a new play for Roaring Epiphany Production Company. A few months later, "Hugo Saves Christmas …in May!" was born. The play centers around a year-round

Christmas store that is going out of business. One character is the employee (who is Jewish) whose mom owns the store. She doesn't really understand the year-round obsession with Christmas. The other character is a longtime customer (Hugo) who is devastated to learn of the store's closing.

There is something about Christmas that makes folks feel happy, safe, and loved. In a world where it feels like something horrible happens in the news daily, it's no wonder that Christmas season unofficially starts earlier every year, with carols starting on the radio sometimes in late October.

However, for Jews in America, it's a different time. Christmas season is a nationwide reminder of their "otherness." I experienced both these worlds firsthand. Raised Jewish with a Catholic stepmother, I celebrated both holidays growing up. I also went to college in Williamsburg, Virginia, where I met my future wife, also Catholic. Christmastime in Williamsburg meant the town was decorated in red and green. If you looked hard enough, you could find a menorah somewhere. A tourist highlight for any parent visiting their child was "The Christmas Mouse," a year-round Christmas store. Even if it was a 98-degree day in May, people would stop by this shop to get their dose of Christmas cheer.

Roaring Epiphany Production Company is a non-profit theater company dedicated to inclusion and bringing people together. Hugo Saves Christmas…in May! is a play about that: two people from different backgrounds, coming together and connecting through shared experiences.

PUBLISHER NOTE: "Hugo Saves Christmas…in May!" by Steven Hayet is a full-length play. We rarely produce full-length plays on the podcast, but this one had just the right amount of charm and we knew we'd have fun producing it. With that in mind, we unfortunately couldn't fit the script for a full-length play in this anthology, but the full script is available at Ghost Light Publications (ghostlightpubs.com).

For licensing rights to this play, please contact info@ghostlightpubs.com.

Episode 4.4
PLAYING WITH DOLLS
(Release date: June 26, 2023)

Written by John Mabey.

Originally written as a stage play but premiered as an audio play on the Gather by the Ghost Light podcast before any stage productions.

Synopsis: Two men exchange dolls in an alleyway, a simple trade that isn't so simple.

<u>Audio Play Production</u>
Produced and directed by Jonathan Cook.
Cast: Ryan Abel (Carl); and Sean Moton (Gregory).
Music Cues: "Wag the Tale" by Roie Shpigler.

Author (John Mabey) commentary: This play was inspired by a similar event in my childhood between my mother and another mother at a toy shop. I decided to broaden the world of the play with fathers in order to explore and subvert traditional depictions of masculinity. Also at the heart of this play is the way men sometimes struggle to form friendships in adulthood, and how the unexpected in life can open so many beautiful opportunities.

For licensing rights to this play, contact the playwright directly at johnemabey@gmail.com.

SCRIPT: PLAYING WITH DOLLS

CHARACTERS

GREGORY...	Male, Black, 20s/30s
CARL...	Male, white, 20s/30s

SETTING

An alleyway behind a toy store.

OPENING MUSIC CUE:
"WAG THE TAIL"

CITY AMBIENCE.

FOOTSTEPS APPROACH.

CARL:	(HUSHED VOICE) Hey. Do you got it?
GREGORY:	We don't have to whisper.
CARL:	Right. Sorry.
	SOUND OF SHOPPING BAGS.
	It's not like it's a racial thing.
GREGORY:	Of course it is.
CARL:	I do have black friends.
GREGORY:	(SARCASTIC) Me too. I just call them "friends".
CARL:	I just came to this toy store for a doll - didn't think I'd get a black one is all.
GREGORY:	So a white doll is a 'doll' and a black doll is a 'black doll.'
CARL:	Don't make me out to be the

	bad guy. You wanted a doll that's a different color too.
GREGORY:	Can we get on with this?

A BAG CRINKLES AS HE
PULLS OUT THE DOLL.

CARL:	So, um, how old's your kid? Mine's maybe 7.
GREGORY:	'Maybe?'
CARL:	I'm not good with birthdays, ages.
GREGORY:	Mine's 7 years, 3 months and 4 days.
CARL:	You got a good head for numbers.
GREGORY:	Not really. I just love my kid. (BEAT) I didn't mean it like that - I'm sure you do too. I just meant - look, we don't need to make conversation. Just... I'll give you this doll, you give me that one.
CARL:	Right. Sure thing.

THEY EXCHANGE THE
DOLLS.

You hear a fight broke out in the store last week 'cus they ran out of 'em? Watched the clip on the news. Makes sense they got rules now.

GREGORY:	They could at least let parents choose - select - the doll they want.
CARL:	Yours watch the cartoon, too?

CARL HUMS THE THEME
SONG. GREGORY JOINS IN.

16

GREGORY: Ugh, that theme song.

CARL: Wouldn't be surprised if the mafia was behind it all.

GREGORY: What?

CARL: It's true. They're always behind the big money scams. I'm not in the mafia but, you know, still got connections.

GREGORY: Huh?

CARL: On my mom's side. She grew up across the street from a family in the Bronx. A limo with a chauffeur would drive their little girl and my mom to and from the park. A limo. Can you believe it? But we were never connected, not directly. Maybe my grandparents were 'cus they immigrated from the south of Italy - can't remember the city, I mean 'village.' It was tiny, but anyone comin' over was somehow connected. Like they knew somebody who knew somebody. (BEAT) Does, um, your kid have a lot of dolls?

GREGORY: (ANNOYED) Look, my daughter is expecting this so -

CARL: Mine has just one at home. Hides it under the bed - thinks we don't know it's there. Not sure how it even got in the house, maybe snuck it in.

GREGORY: Well it's nice you're getting her another.

CARL: 'Him.' It's for my boy.

<u>PAUSE.</u>

That's not weird, right? I just, you know - I dunno.

GREGORY: Kids like all kinds of things at different ages, it doesn't necessarily mean - anything.

CARL: Like what?

GREGORY: Maybe this is something you should talk about with your friends.

CARL: I'm not tellin' my friends.

GREGORY: And a stranger is somehow better?

CARL: Yeah. That's how you hear the truth.

GREGORY: I'm sure he's fine. Your boy. (BEAT) When I was young, I liked to dance.

CARL: But I'm guessin' you never dressed-up dolls and made 'em twirl.

GREGORY: No.

CARL: I don't wanna let him down. Have him look back in 20 or 30 years, say it's all my fault. Like I encouraged it.

GREGORY: Encouraged what?

CARL: I'm not a homophobe. I'm not. I got gay friends, too.

GREGORY: You need to stop pointing those things out.

CARL: We just want him to have as easy a life as possible. My Maggie, this morning she threw out the other one - the one under his bed. You

	should've seen the look on his face.
GREGORY:	Sad?
CARL:	Worse.
GREGORY:	I don't know what you want me to say. (BEAT) I'm sure I'm making a lot of mistakes as a dad, but letting my daughter try the things she enjoys isn't one of them.
CARL:	You sound like a shrink, no offence.
GREGORY:	That's not an insult.
CARL:	Just easy to talk to, all I meant.
GREGORY:	It's actually nice to have an adult conversation for once. I have so few.
CARL:	You a stay-at-home dad?
GREGORY:	(DEFENSIVE) No. Well – yes, but it's just temporary.
CARL:	No shame in it, goin' on 2 years myself. I'm Carl.
GREGORY:	Gregory.

<u>BEAT.</u>

I could keep it for you – the doll. For your boy. When you want to give it to him, just come by, pick it up.

CARL:	Yeah?
GREGORY:	Let me see your phone. I'll add my number.

<u>HE TAPS NUMBERS ON THE PHONE.</u>

CARL:	Do you want mine, too? My

	number?
GREGORY:	For what?
CARL:	Dunno. In case you wanna check-in, update me on how it's goin.'
GREGORY:	I don't expect there will be any updates with the doll.
CARL:	Not about the doll.
GREGORY:	Then why would I call?
CARL:	I'm askin' if you wanna hang out sometime! Grab a beer.
GREGORY:	Oh.
CARL:	(EMBARRASED) It's okay, never mind.
GREGORY:	No!
CARL:	Yeah, I got it. You're not interested.
GREGORY:	I meant 'no' as in 'no I don't mind.'
CARL:	Wow, don't I feel special.
GREGORY:	I'm saying I'd like to - hang out sometime. With you.

MUSIC CUE:
"WAG THE TAIL"

CARL:	(PLAYFUL) Jesus, that was difficult. You always play so hard to get?

PHONE TYPING AND THEN
TEXT ALERT.

	Just texted you. That's me.
GREGORY:	Do you play chess?
CARL:	Not so much. How 'bout bowling?

GREGORY: Eh. I like movies.

CARL: Me too! We can catch a movie.

GREGORY: Great. Maybe sometime next
              month? Or after that is fine
              too.

CARL: Yeah, whenever is good.

GREGORY: Down the road - sometime.

CARL: Cool.

GREGORY: Cool.

CARL: I'll see you around then.

GREGORY: Sounds good.

                        BEAT.

                        NEITHER WALKS AWAY.

                        GREGORY CLEARS THROAT.

              Hey. You hungry?

CARL: Starving.

GREGORY: Come on, you been to that new
              burger joint on 8th?

                        FOOTSTEPS AS THEY BOTH
                        WALK AWAY TOGETHER.

CARL: The one with the big neon
              sign?

GREGORY: That's the one.

CARL: Nah. I didn't think they were
              open yet. How is it?

GREGORY: Man, their burgers will
              change your life.

              END OF PLAY

____

Episode 4.5
A TRAGEDY OF OWLS
(Release date: June 30, 2023)

Written by John Mabey.

Originally premiered as a stage play at the Thalia Arts Company in Norwich, UK in May 2023. Directed by Daria Mazzocchio. Original cast – Jamie McClean (Willem Arondeus); and Stella von Koskull (Lau Mazreil).

Synopsis: After a successful anti-Nazi attack, two co-conspirators meet in prison - one free and one facing death. Both have an urgent but opposing plea for the other.

<u>Audio Play Production</u>
Produced and directed by Jonathan Cook.
Cast: Jonathan Cook (Willem Arondeus); and Amy Patton (Lau Mazreil/Narrator).
Music cues: "Bait" by DaniHaDani.

Author (John Mabey) commentary: This play is a historical piece that takes place during WWII. It's a dramatic interpretation of real people and events in a prison located in Amsterdam, The Netherlands. Two members of the Dutch resistance, one an attorney and the other captured by the Nazis, have an urgent request for each other at their very last encounter. The play not only explores homophobia and resistance to the Nazi regime, but also friendship, love, and social justice.

I lived overseas for nearly a decade, and my time living in Amsterdam especially was so formative. And although separated by time, the real-life events of this play all took place within close proximity to where I lived. The anti-Nazi bombing of the civil registry office was located down the street from my apartment, and I also volunteered for the queer Dutch organization where the attorney in this play worked. The area was so rich in poignant history as my apartment was also just down the block from the Anne Frank House as well.

The characters in this play face horrific obstacles and realities that I can only imagine. And it's a privilege to celebrate their sacrifices and honor their memories. At the heart of the tragedy within this play is also a love story, and I believe it's important to tell the truths of the past while also celebrating that love.

For licensing rights to this play, contact the playwright directly at johnemabey@gmail.com.

SCRIPT: A TRAGEDY OF OWLS

CHARACTERS

WILLEM ARONDEUS...   40s / Man / Dutch, white /
                       member of the Dutch
                       resistance.

LAU MAZIREL...   30s / Woman / Dutch, white
                       / Attorney

SETTING

June 1943.
The Netherlands. A prison.

OPENING MUSIC CUE:
"BAIT"

CELL DOOR OPENS.

CLINK OF HANDCUFFS.

WILLEM GRUNTS IN PAIN.

LAU: Hold still.

WILLEM: Nothing gets done when we hold still.

LAU: Quiet.

WILLEM: Why? My fate is certain. And short.

LAU: I just prefer modesty.

WILLEM LAUGHS AND THEN GRUNTS IN PAIN.

It hurts when you laugh?

WILLEM: And breathe.

LAU: Even your wounds have wounds. It's not right. In the trial –

WILLEM: Nothing is right anymore. Laws are a joke.

LAU: Laws are my life.

WILLEM: The law is what you do, what happened that night is who you are.

LAU: We are all many things.

WILLEM: And right now are you 'friend' or 'attorney?'

LAU: There's not much time and I need something.

WILLEM: As 'friend' or 'attorney?'

LAU: Everything's intertwined.

WILLEM: So you're not answering my question.

LAU: I just did. But you never

	listen, even when it's more than your life I'm trying to save. Come here. Let me clean your face.
WILLEM:	Shouldn't bother. The Nazis toss bruised fruit whether it's washed or not.
LAU:	So much will be washed away in the end.
WILLEM:	Unless we make it known.

<u>BEAT.</u>

LAU:	It's okay to be frightened.
WILLEM:	None of this is coming from fear.
LAU:	We don't have the luxury of lies today.
WILLEM:	I'm only frightened for others.
LAU:	Like Sjoerd?
WILLEM:	I've never heard that name.
LAU:	We're running out of time, and that's the second time you've lied. Possibly third.
WILLEM:	Leave.
LAU:	They already know.
WILLEM:	He was nowhere near the bombing.
LAU:	Willem, they already know. Everything. (BEAT) The two of you. But there's a chance for him to live.
WILLEM:	To 'live' or to 'have a life?'
LAU:	They're the same.

WILLEM: Invisible cages are still
               cages.

LAU: If you and he could simply
               renounce any sort of intimate
               —

               WILLEM LAUGHS AGAIN AND
               THEN GRIMACES IN PAIN.

               Was it worth it?

WILLEM: Do you mean bombing the Nazi
               records, my relationship with
               Sjoerd, or the laugh?

LAU: Goodbye, Willem.

               LAU FOOTSTEPS AS SHE
               WALKS TOWARD THE EXIT.

WILLEM: Yes it was. All of it.

               SHE STOPS WALKING.

               And before you leave I need
               something, too.

LAU: From 'friend' or 'attorney?'

WILLEM: Sjoerd. Is he...

               LAU FOOTSTEPS AS SHE
               WALKS BACK TO HIM.

LAU: Looking like you? Yes. But
               less combative.

WILLEM: He rarely speaks anyway.

LAU: And right now he can barely
               move his lips. They never
               heal quickly when split.

WILLEM: You need to deliver a
               message.

LAU: Make it short, I have no
               tools for writing. Even had
               to remove my hairpin before
               coming in your cell.

WILLEM: No small mercies.

LAU: What do you want him to know?

WILLEM: Not him... it's for the court. I need you to confirm that yes, I am what they say.

LAU: Willem, you clearly don't mean -

WILLEM: A homosexual. And so is Sjoerd. And neither of us were cowards.

> LAU LAUGHS. THE LAUGH IS COMPLEX, NOT A HAPPY ONE.

LAU: They beat you harder than I thought.

WILLEM: I don't expect you to understand.

LAU: But you expect me to be an accomplice to his death.

WILLEM: We're both already gone.

LAU: He doesn't need to be. The evidence is weaker.

WILLEM: The sooner you admit it's out of your hands -

LAU: You know better than anyone what these hands have done. What they can do. What they've already risked.

WILLEM: Who was it?

LAU: No one betrayed you.

WILLEM: Then Sjoerd would be far, far away from here.

LAU: There was a notebook, discovered when they searched your apartment. One you tried

	to burn.
WILLEM:	Tried?
LAU:	Some things are very difficult to destroy.
WILLEM:	I betrayed myself, then. All of us.
LAU:	If you truly believe that, help me now. Deny there was ever a relationship between you two... of that sort.
WILLEM:	When I first met him on the side of the road, Sjoerd was crouching in tears.
LAU:	I already know this story.
WILLEM:	Not the most important part.
LAU:	Willem, the guards will return any –
WILLEM:	I discovered this frail, tiny man holding another frail, tiny creature... cradled to his breast. Neither seemed to have long to live. Wings crushed, eyes wide. Outcasts.
LAU:	Willem, focus.
WILLEM:	This stranger, cradling a baby owl, as war raged all around. And I held my discovery as he held his. A tiny act of courage that sparked a love that lit a fuse that helped thousands to live.
LAU:	The world doesn't want to know such things, Willem. It never will.
WILLEM:	Not as outcasts. But just imagine if we defined

	ourselves? That's what I'm asking.
LAU:	You won't have to live with what you're asking. I will.
WILLEM:	But I won't die knowing we'll just be erased. (BEAT) I woke suddenly... there was a sound outside our bedroom window. Someone moving in the darkness. I gripped the knife as Sjoerd and I went outside. Suddenly we saw it... in the trees. Then another. I swear there was two, then three, then four, then... so many. Surrounding us. I knew what it meant. We've already said our goodbyes.
LAU:	It's rare to see so many owls. Perhaps it was all a dream.
WILLEM:	The dream was everything that came before.
LAU:	'Parliament.' It's called a 'parliament of owls.'
WILLEM:	Terrible name.
LAU:	And yet.
WILLEM:	I wonder what they'd call themselves if given the chance, too. (BEAT) Help me, Lau.
LAU:	800,000 identity cards were destroyed that day, thousands of Jews escaped. But no one will ever celebrate that a homosexual... even several... did anything brave. Let alone believe it.
WILLEM:	But you'll know.

LAU: I'm no one. Not even very good at my job, based on today.

WILLEM: We are all many things, remember?

LAU: I'm not sure I still believe that.

WILLEM: An act of courage anyway.

LAU: It's hard being courageous when you're frightened. Terrified.

WILLEM: Maybe they actually look the same.

LAU: Since when?

WILLEM: Since you. (BEAT) Let it be known.

                        LAU'S FOOTSTEPS WALK TO THE CELL DOOR.

                        THE CELL DOOR OPENS.

                        SCENE TRANSITIONS SO-

                EPILOGUE

NARRATOR: Willem Arondeus and Sjoerd Bakker were both executed a month later on July 1, 1943. After the Netherlands was liberated in 1945, the Dutch government awarded the entire group of resistance fighters a posthumous medal. But due to homophobia, the contributions of Willem, Sjoerd, and the rest of its openly LGBT members were largely erased from public acknowledgment.

In the 1980s, these LGBT resistance fighters were finally given full recognition. They were posthumously awarded the Resistance Memorial Cross as well as recognized as Righteous Among the Nations by Yad Vashem (Israel's official memorial to Holocaust victims). Lau Mazirel lived for another 30 years. She dedicated her career to resistance activities throughout WWII, even getting arrested herself in 1944 for rescuing Jewish children on deportation trains.

After the war, she became a leader in the fight for LGBT rights

<u>END OF PLAY</u>

Episode 4.6
WHEEL OF FORTUNE REVERSED
(Release date: July 13, 2023)

Written by Scott C. Sickles.

Originally premiered as a stage play produced by Traffic Jam Theatre Co. in Savannah, Georgia in June 2023. Directed by Ryan Krewer. Original cast – Ethan Brooks Baker (Michael); and Emma Starbird (Death).

Synopsis: Death has come for Michael, but he has a bucket list that only the Grim Reaper can fulfill.

<u>Audio Play Production</u>
Produced by Jonathan Cook.
Cast: Robert J. LeBlanc (Michael); and Dana Hall (Death).
Music cues: None.

Author (Scott C. Sickles) commentary: Every year since 2020, a playwrights' collective I belong to holds its Secret Santa Title Swap. It's exactly what it sounds like: participating writers offer up a title and are gifted one in return. From there, we write a play to go with the title we received. I was gifted "Wheel of Fortune Reversed" by Emily McClain.

For weeks, I had no idea what the play would be about. Then I watched the opening scene from Ingmar Bergman's "The Seventh Seal" and the train of thought went something like: chess came with death, death is a tarot card, what if someone who saw death in their tarot reading ended up playing chess with death... but who? Then I thought of my friend Michael. After many tumultuous years, Michael found a career path that fulfilled him, met the love of his life, and as he put it "finally got everything he ever wanted" and was then diagnosed with cancer. He was one of the most talented actors I ever had the gift of working with and a friend I could tell anything to. This play is for him. I hope he has found peace.

For licensing rights to this play, contact the Barbara Hogenson agency, Inc. BHogenson@aol.com • 646-256-6641.

SCRIPT: WHEEL OF FORTUNE REVERSED

CHARACTERS

MICHAEL...   Late 30s or older. Any race, gender, ability.

DEATH...   A classic depiction of death: pale white face dressed in black, scythe optional. (Imagined as much like Death in Ingmar Bergman's The Seventh Seal as possible, but you do you.) Any adult age, race, gender, ability.

SETTING

SCENE - A rocky shore. A limbo. Between life and Death. Possibly Sweden.

TIME - Right near the end.

OCEAN SHORE AMBIENCE - WAVES, SEAGULLS, ETC.

FOOTSTEPS IN THE SAND.

MICHAEL: Whoa!!! Oh... Hello you!

DEATH: I take it I need no introduction?

MICHAEL: Do you ever?

DEATH: (SHRUGS) Meh. People...

MICHAEL: I hear you. Actually, I've been wondering when you'd show up.

DEATH: Here I am. Are you prepared?

MICHAEL: Physically? I don't have much choice. Emotionally...? (BEAT) I think I'm good to go.

DEATH: Very well, then.

AN OTHERWORDLY SWELL BEGINS.

MICHAEL: Before you do that...

THE SWELL ABRUPTLY ENDS.

I have a few requests.

DEATH: (SIGHS) Of course you do.

MICHAEL: You play chess, right?

DEATH: Not this again.

MICHAEL: Please?

DEATH: You do know I always win.

MICHAEL: Not this time! Ta da!

A SWOOSH AS HE UNCOVERS A CHESS BOARD.

I've got the board all set up and everything.

DEATH: Really? Are you some kind of chess prodigy?

MICHAEL: Not at all, I'm quite

	terrible! Which is why I propose... (DRAMATIC PAUSE) We don't play to win. We play... to lose.
DEATH:	So if you capture my king?
MICHAEL:	I die.
DEATH:	And if by some freak chance I capture yours?
MICHAEL:	I live the rest of my life.
DEATH:	You've already done that.
MICHAEL:	Then what do you have to lose?
DEATH:	(SIGHS) Sure, why not?
MICHAEL:	Fantastic! Now, I'll mix these up behind my back and we can see who goes first. Left hand or right?
DEATH:	Left.
MICHAEL:	And naturally you've picked... White... Huh. Has that ever happened before?
DEATH:	About fifty-fifty.
MICHAEL:	Oh. I guess that makes sense. Okay, I guess I go first.

    HE MOVES A CHESS PIECE.

Your move.

    DEATH MOVES A CHESS PIECE.

A pawn? Not a knight? You are full of surprises. All righty then...

    MORE CHESS PIECES ARE MOVED.

Okay your—

DEATH: Checkmate.

MICHAEL: What?

DEATH: I mean you.

MICHAEL: Wow, you're right.

DEATH: Now, shall we-

MICHAEL: Best of three?

DEATH: (SIGHS) Fine.

            MICHAEL RESETS THE
            CHESS BOARD.

MICHAEL: Thank you. For indulging me.

DEATH: It's no problem.

            CHESS PIECES ARE MOVED
            AS THEY TALK.

MICHAEL: I was hoping you'd be cool
            about it. I mean, you never
            know what to expect from
            Death, right? You could have
            been a total dick. Or just
            all business. But once the
            pain stopped... Well... It
            didn't really stop as much as
            I was okay with it. But once
            it did, I figured you'd be...
            Do you... Do you know about
            my life?

DEATH: Not really.

MICHAEL: Huh? I thought you'd know
            everything.

DEATH: Why would I need to?

MICHAEL: Fair enough.

DEATH: Why?

MICHAEL: It's just... It wasn't great,
            my life. Not overall. It was
            very lonely. Very angry. When
            it wasn't sad. And then, I

went to this fortune teller. And that's the first time I saw you. Harbinger of change, and damn were you right!

DEATH: That wasn't me. That was just a card.

MICHAEL: I know but... timing is everything. And after I saw you, I landed my dream job. I moved into a place I finally felt at home in. Met the love of my life, got married. I finally had everything I wanted. I wondered, what could happen next? So, I went to another fortune teller and...

DEATH: Did you see me again?

MICHAEL: If only. No, I got the Tower, the Hanged Man, and the Wheel of Fortune. All reversed. The first two are always bad news but the Wheel... it could have been good news, but instead it was like confirmation that there was no hope. I have to admit, I was shook. Of course, it's just superstition, right? Entertainment? Then I got the headaches. Then the scans. I guess when you run out of things to want, you start getting things you don't. I had to leave my job. Moved out of my house into hospice. But love... Love stayed with me. Love eased the agony. Sure, I might not have cared as much about the pain, but I also wouldn't have fought so hard against it. Love is

	holding my hand right now. I can actually still feel it... the warmth of their grip... it's-
DEATH:	Checkmate.
MICHAEL:	Exactly! Oh. You meant... I win again?
DEATH:	That's best of three. Sorry. I held out as long as I could.
MICHAEL:	Thank you. That was kind. Question: In all the chess games over all the millennia, has anyone else ever played you to lose?
DEATH:	In all the chess games over all the millennia, do you really think you're the first?
MICHAEL:	Yeah, I guess the odds were-
DEATH:	I'm messing with you; you totally are.
MICHAEL:	Really?! You're not just saying that-
DEATH:	I'm Death. Why would I lie?
MICHAEL:	Awesome! High five!
	FOOTSTEPS AS HE GOES IN FOR A HIGH-FIVE, BUT THEN HE STOPS.
	Wait! If we high-five, do I, like... is that it?
DEATH:	Well...
MICHAEL:	We can just high-five ourselves.
DEATH:	Sure.

<u>MICHAEL HIGH-FIVES</u>
<u>HIMSELF.</u>

I have a question. If you knew the game would end this way, then why...

MICHAEL: Honestly? I just want to tell people I played chess with Death.

DEATH: You're dying. Who is there to tell?

MICHAEL: Folks in the afterlife. There is an afterlife, isn't there?

DEATH: There is peace.

MICHAEL: Like a peace I'll experience and be happy with? Or like an oblivion I'm not aware of because I no longer exist?

DEATH: Are you afraid of oblivion?

MICHAEL: Hell yes, I'm afraid of... Actually... I think what I'm afraid of is being aware of my own oblivion.

DEATH: Awareness of oblivion isn't truly oblivion, is it?

MICHAEL: True...

DEATH: What do you want your afterlife to be?

MICHAEL: (AT A LOSS) I...

DEATH: Take a moment. Ponder the question. Let it answer itself in your head. Look forward to that.

MICHAEL: And that's what'll happen? I get it. You could tell me but then you'd have to kill me.

DEATH: Why does it matter?

MICHAEL: What? The nothingness? I guess because if there's nothing... after everything everybody has ever gone through, all the love and anger, the good and the bad, if after all the something there's... I don't know. I just hate the idea that inspirational posters with kittens and rainbows were right about living in the moment.

DEATH: You didn't live in the moment?

MICHAEL: About fifty-fifty. When I did, the moment was either too short or too long. I could never get it right.

DEATH: Look on the bright side. It's not a problem anymore.

MICHAEL: You don't get invited to many dinner parties, do you?

DEATH: Invited? No.

MICHAEL: I see what you did there.

DEATH: Any other last requests?

MICHAEL: Actually, I have two more bucket list items. But I have to make sure... (GATHERS THOUGHTS) Okay, so what happens if you kiss me?

DEATH: Well... You die...

MICHAEL: And if you embrace me?

DEATH: You die.

MICHAEL: What happens if I don't die?

DEATH: You will.

MICHAEL:	But do I have to?
DEATH:	What are you asking?
MICHAEL:	Can you kiss me, then embrace me... and then I die?
DEATH:	Oh. Huh.
MICHAEL:	It's just that I've heard all my life about the "kiss of death" and "death's cold embrace..."
DEATH:	Do you really want a cold embrace?
MICHAEL:	Honestly, I could use a hug right now and beggars can't be choosers, so...
DEATH:	Come here.

<u>OTHERWORLDLY CHIMES.</u>

<u>A CLOAK SWOOSHES AROUND MICHAEL.</u>

MICHAEL:	Thank you. Who knew Death was such a gentle kisser-Oh.
DEATH:	What?
MICHAEL:	I don't feel their hand anymore.
DEATH:	I'm sorry.
MICHAEL:	It's all right. The peace... That's happening...
DEATH:	Well, then... We should get to the embrace-

<u>FOOTSTEPS IN THE SAND.</u>

MICHAEL:	Wait.

<u>PAUSE AS MICHAELS SAVORS THE PEACE.</u>

Okay. I'm ready. Bring it in.

<u>A WAVE CRASHES OVER THEM.</u>

<u>OTHERWORDLY AMBIENCE.</u>

You're warm.

DEATH: That's not just me.

MICHAEL: What do you...? Oh. So that's...

DEATH: Love holding onto you while they let you go.

MICHAEL: I didn't think that... when I went... I'd be able to feel that... How lucky.

<u>OTHERWORDLY RISER AS DEATH TAKES MICHEAL.</u>

<u>END OF PLAY.</u>

Episode 4.7
TOOTH OR DARE
(Release date: July 31, 2022)

Written by Emily McClain.

Originally premiered as a stage play at 6th Street Theatre (Racine, WI) in January 2021 as part of the Over Our Head Players[6] Snowdance Theatre Festival.

Synopsis: Don't piss off the tooth fairy. Just don't do it.

<u>Audio Play Production</u>
Produced and directed by Jonathan Cook.
Cast: Andrew Jones (Andrew); Jamie Johnston Turner (Lydia); and Kayla Gardner (Tooth Fairy).
Music cues: "A Pinch of Magic" by Jakub Pietras.

Author (Emily McClain) commentary: This play was directly inspired by my daughter Eleanor, who pulled her own tooth and didn't tell anybody and was extremely upset with the Tooth Fairy when she failed to deliver the following morning. The resulting conversation with her led to me "emailing" the Tooth Fairy to find out when she was going to make good on her promise. Modern parenting is a surreal adventure and I was glad to use this play to work through the trauma of this experience.

For licensing rights to this play, contact the playwright directly at emilymcclain234@gmail.com.

SCRIPT: TOOTH OR DARE

CHARACTERS

ANDREW...	40's male.
LYDIA...	40's female.
TOOTH FAIRY...	The immortal magical being.

SETTING

A bedroom.
The present.

	MUSIC CUE: "A PINCH OF MAGIC"
	ANDREW/LYDIA SNORE.
	TOOTH FAIRY'S MAGICAL ENTRANCE.
TOOTH FAIRY:	Ew. Well, this looks like the place. (TO THE SLEEPING ANDREW AND LYDIA) Are you the parents of Natalie Gillis?
	ANDREW GROANS IN HIS SLEEP.
	TOOTH FAIRY SMACKS HIM A FEW TIMES WITH HER POUCH. MAGICAL JINGLES.
	Hey! Buddy! Look alive!
ANDREW:	(WAKING UP ABRUPTLY) Ow! Ow! Hey! What the-
LYDIA:	(STILL GROGGY) Andrew, shh...
TOOTH FAIRY:	Is your daughter named

	Natalie Gillis?
ANDREW:	Oh my God! Who are you!
LYDIA:	What's going- AH!

ANDREW AND LYDIA PANIC.

BED SHEETS SHIFT AROUND AS THEY FREAK OUT.

TOOTH FAIRY:	Are you done?
ANDREW:	Who are you?!? How did you get in our house?
LYDIA:	Andrew! Call the police!
TOOTH FAIRY:	I'm going to ask again- and I really hate repeating myself, so please just answer the question this time instead of screaming. Are you. The parents. Of Natalie Gillis. Aged 7. Lost 4 teeth: two top incisors, one bottom incisor and a canine, bottom left-
ANDREW:	How do you know our daughter's name? How do you know about her dental records? What the hell is going on?
LYDIA:	Oh my God, have you done something to Natalie?
TOOTH FAIRY:	No! More like she's done something to me! Look!

TOOTH FAIRY PUTS A BRIGHT SCREEN IN LYDIA'S FACE. BED SHEETS SHUFFLE AROUND AS SHE'S BLINDED.

| LYDIA: | Get that out of my face, is that a cell phone? |
| TOOTH FAIRY: | No, it's not a cell phone! |

This is my Toothberry! And if you look at the screen, you can see it shows the Magical Beings Satisfaction Rankings! My MBS Overall Score! You look!

<u>SHE SHOVES THE DEVICE INTO ANDREW'S FACE.</u>

ANDREW: Sorry, it's a little close, and bright- Let me get my glasses. There. Okay... so, what exactly am I looking at here?

TOOTH FAIRY: My score- my satisfaction score has sat in the enviable position of 93% overall satisfaction for the last DECADE. I have DOMINATED. Beating out the Bunny, leaping over Leprechauns, catapulting over Cupid, year after year after year. I was second to only Santa himself!

LYDIA: Look, I don't know what you're talking about but you need to get out of my house before I call the police, you sparkling psycho!

ANDREW: Are you... are you really the Tooth Fairy?

TOOTH FAIRY: And now just look at it! 71%! A seventy-one!

LYDIA: Andrew, call the police!

ANDREW: Okay. I am!

<u>TWO NUMBERS DIAL.</u>

TOOTH FAIRY: Ah, ah, ah.

<u>MAGICAL SWOOSH.</u>

<u>CELL PHONE IS LAUNCHED</u>

<u>OUT OF THE WINDOW.</u>

<u>GLASS SHATTERS.</u>

ANDREW: Woah!

LYDIA: Why'd you throw your phone out the window?!

ANDREW: I didn't throw it! She did something with her sparkly demon powers!

TOOTH FAIRY: Listen up! We're dealing with this. Damn it, would you look at this, I'm even behind the ELF on the SHELF! Are you kidding me with this right now? And it's all because of YOUR daughter!

ANDREW: What has Natalie got to do with any of this?

LYDIA: Andrew! She's a crazy person!

TOOTH FAIRY: (READING FROM HER DEVICE IN A NASALLY MOCKING VOICE) "Two days ago, I lost a tooth while I was eating an apple at school. I brought it home and put it under my pillow like always and the next morning there wasn't any money and the tooth was still there! My parents said that the Tooth Fairy must have gotten "unavoidably detained" and they were sure she would come the next night. I think this is unacceptable service and expect better from the Tooth Fairy. Perhaps she is losing her edge? Is it time for retirement? 0/10 Would Not Recommend. Natalie Gillis, age 7."

LYDIA: Ok... wait a second...

TOOTH FAIRY: She gave me a ZERO. In one
                 fell swoop she tanked my
                 record. It's... God. I mean,
                 ridiculous, right? Like, that
                 algorithm has got to be
                 flawed, for one bad rating to
                 have that kind of impact, but
                 all the same-

ANDREW: Um, okay, listen, Ms. Fairy,
                 uh, Your Fairyness-

TOOTH FAIRY: TF is fine.

ANDREW: What... TF? Sure, okay, TF.
                 We... we did tell Natalie
                 that when we realized we'd
                 both forgotten-

LYDIA: No, YOU forgot.

ANDREW: Do you really want to do this
                 right now?

LYDIA: I just want everyone to be
                 clear on the facts of the
                 situation.

ANDREW: (OVERLAPPING) No, you just
                 want to blame me-

LYDIA: You said you were going to
                 put the money under the
                 pillow!

ANDREW: Hey, yeah, wait a minute...
                 We do. WE put the money under
                 the pillow... And buy the
                 presents from Santa... and
                 hide the eggs. We do that
                 stuff... Right?

LYDIA: Yes, of course! We're good
                 parents, you just dropped the
                 ball this one time and-

ANDREW: Wow, you never miss a chance
                 to- no, what I was saying

was, we are the ones who do the work for all these holiday people- but you're saying you... like this score is about you? As if you are the one doing the work?

TOOTH FAIRY: I don't really have time to get into the particulars of my business with you, but a long time ago it became clear that unless I was going to be operating on some kind of deficit-spending model for all eternity, yeah, I needed to outsource the labor portion of my business to parents. We all made the transition together.

LYDIA: We?

TOOTH FAIRY: The International Consortium of Supernatural Beings and Otherworldly Phenomena. So yeah. You people, as parents do the bulk of the work. But you are trading on my BRAND, you see. You reflect on my image. And quite frankly, Lydia and Andrew, your work in this area leaves a LOT to be desired.

LYDIA: Excuse me?

TOOTH FAIRY: You heard me. You need to make this right. Tell your daughter the truth about who really forgot to perform the sacred office of the Tooth Fairy. And get her to take down this horrible review.

ANDREW: We can't tell her that we're the ones that forgot!

LYDIA: That YOU forgot-

ANDREW: Okay, Lydia, you've made your point!

LYDIA: But he's right. She's only 7! I don't want to tell her that we're the Tooth Fairy. I don't want to spoil that part of childhood for her. And I think it's pretty monstrous that you'd suggest that.

TOOTH FAIRY: Really?

LYDIA: Yes! As a matter of fact, I've got half a mind to get on that website and leave a review of my own. What do you think of that?

TOOTH FAIRY: You've got half a mind, all right.

ANDREW: Hey now.

TOOTH FAIRY: What kind of 7-year-old writes negative online reviews anyway? Where would she learn a thing like that?

                          ANDREW SNICKERS.

LYDIA: What's wrong with that? She has as much right to express her opinion as anyone else.

ANDREW: She really enjoys it. She's got lots of followers for her Polly Pocket unboxing videos on YouTube.

TOOTH FAIRY: (SARCASTICALLY) Oh wow, I'll be sure to check that out.

ANDREW: Okay, no need to be rude.

LYDIA: I'm not going to ruin my daughter's innocence because you're upset about your Uber score-

TOOTH FAIRY: MBS Score.

LYDIA: Whatever. So just take your hideous glittery handbag and get the hell out of my bedroom!

                MUSIC CUE:
                "A PINCH OF MAGIC"

TOOTH FAIRY: (SIGHING) I was really hoping it wouldn't come to this, I really was. Remember, you've left me no choice.

                MAGICAL JINGLE.

                CRUNCH NOISE.

                ANDREW SCREAMS IN PAIN. AND CONTINUES TO BE IN PAIN THROUGHOUT REST OF SCENE.

LYDIA: Andrew! Andrew, what's wrong?

ANDREW: (IN EXCRUTIATING PAIN) My tooth- MY TOOTH! Oh my God Oh my God make it stop!

                ANDREW IN PAIN, ROLLING AROUND ON BED.

LYDIA: (TO TOOTH FAIRY) Please stop this! Please! We're sorry!

TOOTH FAIRY: That's not good enough.

                ANOTHER MAGICAL JINGLE, FOLLOWED BY ANOTHER CRUNCH, AND THE PAIN INTENSIFIES.

ANDREW: (MOANING PITIFULLY) Ohhhhh... damn it, Lydia, tell her... we'll tell Natalie... ohhhh...

LYDIA: Fine! FINE! We'll tell

	Natalie that we're the ones who are putting the money under her pillow and we screwed up and forgot!
TOOTH FAIRY:	And?
LYDIA:	(MUTTER) And I'll make her take down the review.
TOOTH FAIRY:	Excuse me? Didn't quite catch that?
ANDREW:	Lydia!
LYDIA:	I said I'll make her take down the review! Okay? Happy now? Stop torturing him!

TOOTH FAIRY MAGICAL JINGLE.

ANDREW STOPS MOANING IN PAIN AND SPITS OUT A TOOTH.

	Oh my God, Andrew, is that your tooth? You pulled out his tooth?
TOOTH FAIRY:	That seems like a really unnecessary question. So. I'm guessing we have an agreement, right? You're going to take care of telling Natalie the truth and take down the review? I trust I don't have to come back here?
ANDREW:	Yes! God, yes, we promise! We'll wake her up right now, okay?
TOOTH FAIRY:	Yeah, she must be a pretty heavy sleeper to stay conked out through all your screaming and carrying on... Whew. Good for her. Okay. Well, I guess I'll be on my

	way.
LYDIA:	Wait! What about his tooth? Fix it!
TOOTH FAIRY:	You must have me confused with an oral surgeon. I'm not in the "putting teeth back in" business.
ANDREW:	So what am I supposed to do?
TOOTH FAIRY:	Stick it under your pillow and see if Lydia here gives you a dollar for it. Have a nice evening, folks. Byeeeee!

<u>TOOTH FAIRY'S MAGICAL EXIT.</u>

<u>END OF PLAY.</u>

Episode 4.8
THE DEMON LADY
(Release date: September 1, 2023)

Written by John Patrick Bray.

Originally premiered as a stage play as part of "An Evening of Suspense" with Gardner-Webb University's[7] Theatre Season on April 20, 2023. It was directed by Dr. Christopher Nelson and featured the following cast: Aliah McKennedy (Veronica); Noah Seip (Jeremy); Roman Cotty (Dash); and Faith Augustine (Porch Mouth). The creative team consisted of Richard Horsley (Scenic Design); Elie Brinson (Lighting Design); and Dr. Christopher Nelson (Sound Design).

Synopsis: A couple of friends decide to escape for a weekend and go camping but a sudden storm in the middle of the night destroys their tent and now they are desperately looking for shelter. But what they find instead may just be a little more dangerous than the rain.

<u>Audio Play Production</u>
Produced and directed by Jonathan Cook.
Cast: Audrey Robertson (Veronica); Eric Odom (Jeremy); and Christy Roosma (Dash / Porch Mouth).
Music cues: "Tumannoye Ozero (The Misty Lake)" by Ian Post.

Author (John Patrick Bray) commentary: I wrote "The Demon Lady" as part of a #28PlaysLater event, hosted by Rebecca Holbourn of Dramatic Chaos Productions. My inspiration for this piece was a Japanese Noh Demon play I read in grad school, in which a group of monks visit an old lady in the woods. They find corpses in her closet of all the men she has murdered – she is in fact a demon! The monks chant, releasing the spirits of the deceased, and the demon disappears. (At least, that's my memory of the piece.) I wanted to write a play in which we root for the demon, for the lady in the woods, and for a young woman who feels alone in the world.

For licensing rights to this play, contact the playwright directly at JohnPatrickBray@gmail.com.

SCRIPT: THE DEMON LADY

CHARACTERS

VERONICA...   Maybe 30s, angry at the world.

JEREMY...   Maybe 40s, sad at the world.

DASH...   Probably a Demon Lady. Maybe.

PORCH MOUTH...   A surprise.

SETTING

The front porch of a cabin in the woods.
Not too long ago.

MUSIC CUE:
"THE MISTY LAKE"

THUNDERSTORM
AMBIENCE.

FOOTSTEPS WALK ALONG
THE WET GROUND.

JEREMY: Can't see shit out here.

VERONICA: This storm came outta
                nowhere. Looks like
                there's a trail here. Come
                on.

JEREMY: Wait! Look over there. A
                cabin!

VERONICA: Whoa. That place looks
                creepy as fuck. The dim
                lights in the windows look
                like wicked eyes staring
                us down.

JEREMY: Everything out here looks
                creepy as fuck right now
                but at least there's a
                covered porch at the
                cabin. Maybe they'll let
                us wait this out and stay
                dry.

                        LOUD THUNDERSTRIKE.

                Come on, hurry!

                        FOOTSTEPS RUN
                        THROUGH THE RAIN AND
                        THEN ONTO A WOODEN
                        PORCH AS THE STORM
                        CONTINUES.

                (OUT OF BREATH) There,
                that's a little better.

VERONICA: (OUT OF BREATH) Won't be
                safe.

JEREMY: What?

VERONICA: The camping gear.

JEREMY: If you had just let me
                pack it up –

VERONICA: Are you gonna knock or
                what?

JEREMY: Fine.

                    KNOCKS ON THE CABIN
                    DOOR.

                    Did you see any other
                    campers? Or any camp site
                    roads?

VERONICA: I don't trust it.

JEREMY: What?

VERONICA: The woods. I don't trust
                    'em.

JEREMY: Why did you agree on this
                    trip in the first place?

VERONICA: The places you will go.

JEREMY: What?

VERONICA: Book I read as a kid. The
                    places you will go.

                    THE PORCH CREAKS AS
                    JEREMY WALKS ARUND.

JEREMY: Geez, this place looks
                    even creepier up close.
                    Look at all this rotten
                    wood.

                    THEY HEAR FOOTSTEPS
                    ON THE INSIDE.

VERONICA: Shhh... Someone's coming
                    to the door.

                    THE DOOR CREAKS
                    OPEN.

JEREMY: Hi. I'm so sorry for
                    knocking so late.

DASH: No visitors.

                    DASH CLOSES THE
                    DOOR.

                    JEREMY KNOCKS AGAIN.

JEREMY: Hello!

                   DASH OPENS THE DOOR.

                   We don't want to intrude –

DASH: No solicitors.

                   DASH CLOSES THE DOOR
                   WITH MORE FORCE THIS
                   TIME.

                   THE WINDOW SHADES
                   GET PULLED DOWN.

JEREMY: Great. Now she's also
                   closed the window shades.

                   THUNDERSTRIKE.

                   JEREMY POUNDS ON THE
                   CABIN DOOR.

JEREMY: (LOUDLY) Excuse me, Miss!

VERONICA: Just move.

                   POUNDS ON THE DOOR.

                   Please. We're lost!

                   THE DOOR OPENS.

                   DASH COMES OUT WITH
                   A SHOTGUN.

DASH: I said no visitors!

                   SHE COCKS THE GUN.

JEREMY: Whoa! Whoa. Whoa. Watch it
                   with that shotgun!

DASH: Get off the porch.

VERONICA: Wait! Our tent... a tree
                   fell on our tent... it
                   ripped. The gear... the
                   water... we just... can we
                   just sit on your porch? We
                   don't even have to come
                   inside.

DASH: Don't shoot.

VERONICA: Pardon?

DASH: Usually, people say "don't shoot." And then I shoot.

VERONICA: Well, I won't say it then.

DASH: Say what?

> SILENCE.
>
> THUNDER RUMBLES.

Okay, you're smart. Look, I don't have much. I live out here for a reason. Alone. But you're pretty. Like me when I was younger. And this one. He your husband?

JEREMY: (TOGETHER) No.
VERONICA: (TOGETHER) GOD, NO!

> MUSIC CUE:
> "THE MISTY LAKE"

JEREMY: We're friends. Old friends. We worked at a bagel shop together.

DASH: Bagels?

VERONICA: We just wanted to get away from the world and - Can I put my hands down?

DASH: You may.

VERONICA: Will you lower the gun?

DASH: No.

VERONICA: Okay.

JEREMY: We're just two friends who went camping in the wrong place on the wrong night. Neither of us are actually good at it. We didn't

think about the trees, the
rain, the mosquitoes, -

DASH: The Mountain Lions. The
Bears. The Cannibal Old
Woman.

EERIE STINGER AS
MUSIC ABRUPTLY ENDS.

(BEAT) Heh. I like you.
You're more afraid of
water than you are of me!
Well, then. Might as well
lower the gun.

VERONICA: Thank you.

DASH: You can sit on my porch
until the rain passes. But
just sit quietly. Don't
disturb nothing, you hear
me? Stay real quiet,
disturb nothing.

JEREMY: Do you have any towels?

CABIN DOOR SHUTS.

SLAM!

Never mind.

VERONICA: We have a place to sit
anyway. Shit. I left my
meds in the bag.

JEREMY: What meds?

VERONICA: My Valacyclovir.

JEREMY: Oh. That's the thing for
the um...

VERONICA: The gift that keeps on
giving that Roy left me
with.

JEREMY: Sorry.

VERONICA: It would be nice if all

	this rain would just wash it all away. The past.
JEREMY:	It can't though.
VERONICA:	God. I hate the world.
JEREMY:	The world doesn't think you're too bad.
VERONICA:	You ever want to watch it burn.
JEREMY:	Is that better than drowning?

<u>SILENCE.</u>

	Of course, I do. But not out of anger, just out of... enough, you know?
VERONICA:	I got enough anger for both of us.
JEREMY:	Yeah.
VERONICA:	How come you never got remarried... after?
JEREMY:	How come you never dated... after?
VERONICA:	Come on.
JEREMY:	It's not the big deal it was in the 70s. Medication and such. There's nothing to be ashamed of.
VERONICA:	I'll tell you what. Let me give it to you and you tell me.
JEREMY:	Heh. No way.
VERONICA:	See?
JEREMY:	Because I don't want all that anymore. You know? When I watched her coffin go into the ground and

watched the world swallow her up, I realized I spent my life working. Thinking you know, I'd go to college, and then go to the real world. And work for something. Toward something. With no idea what that something is. But there is no real world. There's just a relentless pursuit of something that doesn't exist, you know? But at least I had her. (BEAT.) I put a padlock on the house, Veronica. I think I'm just going to wander into the woods and let them swallow me up.

VERONICA: And leave me in it? Fuck that. You know, when everyone else is gone, and I mean everyone, it'll just be you and me washing each other's asses at the end of the world. And maybe it'll be better that way. And this time when we put a padlock on the door, we'll be inside first. Because if I got to see that God damn world out there knowing I ain't got a friend in it, I'd rather see it torn to pieces. I'd let the world get swallowed up if I didn't have a friend in it.

JEREMY: So... you're saying you're a little angry?

<u>SHE LAUGHS.</u>

VERONICA: I guess you could say
                that.

                        THEY BOTH LAUGH A
                        LITTLE.

                        THUNDERSTRIKE.

                I was supposed to be on a
                cruise this weekend.

JEREMY: I know.

VERONICA: I still have the damn
                brochures. Caribbean
                Cruise. And Roy was going
                to propose.

JEREMY: I know.

VERONICA: And not give me herpes.
                Shit. I wonder if he's
                spread this joy to any of
                his sidepieces. Oh, the
                places you will go. A
                cruise. Europe.
                Everywhere. You will go
                everywhere. Then
                "everywhere" becomes
                "regular trips to the
                doctor" thanks to life's
                surprises. (BEAT.) I'm
                sorry. I can't believe I
                keep running around this
                circle. You think you have
                your life figured out
                then...

JEREMY: You end up out here with
                me.

VERONICA: Yeah. That part's okay if
                you're fishing for
                compliments.

JEREMY: I think someone saying
                they'd wash my ass when
                I'm old is the best
                compliment I'll ever get.

<u>LOUD THUNDERSTRIKE. VERY CLOSE.</u>

VERONICA: DAMN! That one was close. Maybe if we ask the lady real nice?

<u>JEREMY KNOCKS ON THE DOOR.</u>

JEREMY: (LOUDLY) Ma'am? Ma'am? It's really rough out here.

<u>THE DOOR OPENS.</u>

<u>DASH STEPS OUT.</u>

DASH: Don't call me "Ma'am." It's Dash.

JEREMY: Dash?

DASH: Like a dash of salt. Dash of pepper. Dash.

JEREMY: Or Mrs. Dash?

DASH: There's no Mr. Dash.

JEREMY: I just meant like the, you know... the seasoning?

VERONICA: Can we come in, Dash?

DASH: No.

VERONICA: What if I tell you my name? I'm Veronica.

DASH: That changes everything. No, Veronica.

JEREMY: (SINGING) "Brother Noah, Brother Noah May I come into the Ark of the Lord, For its growing very dark, and it's raining very hard Hallelujah.

DASH: Oh, a Christian! Jewish folks never add the

"Hallelujah."

VERONICA: Are you antisemitic?

DASH: You asking for shelter from the storm?

JEREMY: We're fine out here. We'll be off your porch...

<u>HUGE THUNDERSTRIKE.</u>

...soon.

DASH: You said bagels. I assumed.

JEREMY: Oh. None of us at the bagel shop were Jewish.

VERONICA: Peter was Jewish.

JEREMY: Kellerman. One "n." German, but not Jewish.

VERONICA: Oh. Huh.

DASH: This is fascinating. Good night.

VERONICA: Wait! I gotta pee. Can I pee in one of these buckets?

DASH: As long as you ain't got any of those STI's. Do you?

VERONICA: ...no.

DASH: Are you lying to me? (LONG PAUSE) What about you?

JEREMY: No, I don't have anything like that.

DASH: Then maybe you can use my bathroom. One at a time. The girl first.

VERONICA: Thank you!

<u>VERONICA ENTERS THE</u>

<u>HOUSE.</u>

DASH: You wait. Don't disturb anything.

JEREMY: I won't, I –

<u>THE DOOR CLOSES.</u>

I won't.

<u>NERVOUSLY SINGING TO HIMSELF.</u>

Brother Noah. Brother Noah. May I come into the Ark of the Lord?

<u>THE FLOORBOARD CREAKS AS HE WALKS.</u>

Though it's growing very dark, and it's... huh. Loose board here. Typical old house. Typical old wooden porch. Let's see. Huh. It feels like it wants to come up.

<u>HE PRIES ON THE BOARD TIL IT COMES LOOSE, THEN HE TOSSES IT ASIDE.</u>

I probably shouldn't be doing this. "Don't disturb anything." Jeez, this whole porch is already disturbed. Maybe I can fix it. This one board just needs a little push.

<u>WOOD CRACKS.</u>

Ah, crap. This one is beyond repair. It's rotted like an old tooth. Just came right up. Ew, what is that under there? What are those things?

<u>THUNDERSTRIKE.</u>

Are those bones? OH MY GOD! SKULLS! THOSE ARE HUMAN SKULLS! Oh my God... she really is a cannibal. Oh, God. Oh god, oh god. I gotta get Veronica outta here.

<u>DOOR OPENS.</u>

DASH: Something wrong?

JEREMY: Nope. Thank you.

DASH: You. You can use the bathroom next.

JEREMY: I don't need to.

DASH: You must need to. The bladder of men in the rain.

JEREMY: I don't want to!

DASH: I don't believe that. You wet your pants? Are you a pants-wetter?

JEREMY: No, I'm not an anything. Put the gun down.

DASH: Get in my house. Pee in my can.

JEREMY: Or you'll shoot me?

DASH: Yep.

VERONICA: Jesus! What's wrong with you?

JEREMY: Fine. Fine. I'll... I'll come in.

VERONICA: (ANGRY) It's not like you have to sit. I did wipe up. Jesus.

JEREMY: What?

VERONICA: You're not gonna catch anything, dick!

JEREMY: Veronica, that's not... (TO DASH.) I'll come in. And look at that. The storm seems to be passing. (NERVOUSLY) Hey, Veronica. Why don't you go wait off the porch? Just wait off the porch. I'll be right back.

DASH: Move.

DASH AND JEREMY GO INSIDE.

THE DOOR CLOSES.

MUSIC CUE: "THE MISTY LAKE"

VERONICA: Wait off the porch? In the rain? The hell is wrong with him. I'm not gonna stand out there in the rain.

OLD HOUSE CRUNCHING AND RUMBLING.

THE WIND PICKS UP.

Whoa. Holy shit. The porch is moving!

FOOTSTEPS AS SHE STEPS OFF PORCH.

PORCH MOUTH: Veronica...

VERONICA: Are you talking to me???? The porch is... speaking! Oh my God, it's like a hideous mouth!

THE SHADES OPEN AGAIN.

PORCH MOUTH: I see you.

VERONICA: Windows like eyes...
looking through me...

PORCH MOUTH: Veronica...

VERONICA: It knows my name?

> THE HOUSE
> RUMBLES/LAUGHS.

AHH!!!!

> GUNSHOT IS HEARD
> INSIDE CABIN.

JEREMY?!!! JEREMY!!!!!

> CABIN DOOR SWINGS
> OPEN.

> JEREMY RUNS OUT WITH
> THE GUN.

JEREMY: I got the gun away from
her! She's a killer! Did
you see all those skulls
under the porch! We gotta
get outta here! She killed
them! RUN!

VERONICA: Jeremy, get off the porch!

JEREMY: What? What's going on??

> THE PORCH CRACKS
> OPEN.

Ahh!!!

> THE PORCH SWALLOWS
> JEREMY AS HE SCREAMS
> AND GURGLES.

VERONICA: Oh my god, Jeremy!!!

PORCH MOUTH: She has kept me from
assuming my true form...
from eating...

> THE CABIN SHAKES AND

<table>
<tr><td></td><td>BEGINS TO RISE.</td></tr>
<tr><td></td><td>CABIN DOOR SWINGS OPEN.</td></tr>
<tr><td></td><td>DASH COMES OUT SHAKING A CANNISTER OF HERBS.</td></tr>
<tr><td>DASH:</td><td>Stand back, girl.</td></tr>
<tr><td>VERONICA:</td><td>The house – it's rising out of the ground!</td></tr>
<tr><td></td><td>DASH CONTINUES SHAKING THE HERBS AND THEN SPRINKLES IT ONTO THE PORCH.</td></tr>
<tr><td>DASH:</td><td>GET DOWN, YOU VILE THING! Take your medicine! A dash here, a dash there!</td></tr>
<tr><td></td><td>THE CABIN MOANS AS IT SETTLES BACK TO THE GROUND.</td></tr>
<tr><td></td><td>I warned you and your friend not to disturb anything!</td></tr>
<tr><td>VERONICA:</td><td>What are you sprinkling?</td></tr>
<tr><td>DASH:</td><td>A dash here and a dash there!</td></tr>
<tr><td></td><td>THE HOUSE RUMBLES ONE LAST TIME AND THEN STOPS.</td></tr>
<tr><td></td><td>THE STORM BEGINS TO CALM.</td></tr>
<tr><td></td><td>DASH IS IN PAIN ABOUT TO DIE.</td></tr>
<tr><td></td><td>Idiot. He shot me. That idiot shot me.</td></tr>
<tr><td>VERONICA:</td><td>Jeremy...?</td></tr>
</table>

DASH:

Gone... just bones by now. It swallows them whole and leaves nothing behind. Here. Take this shaker.

<u>SHE HANDS VERONICA THE SHAKER.</u>

It's not enough yet. Sprinkle more to keep it under control. I have more jars of the stuff inside. It's all on you now. You have to be the one to hold it back now. Shake it out all along the wood. Whenever it rumbles, whenever its windows start to look like eyes. Shake it all over the house. Especially the porch. Please, take it! TAKE IT! Or your friend dies in vain. So many have died in vain.

VERONICA:

Okay, I'll... okay...

DASH:

I shouldn't have let you come in. You shouldn't have even waited on the porch. It smelled you. It tasted you. They call me the cannibal. The Demon Lady. But it's this house. She's the demon. And she can walk. She can eat towns. I've been holding her at bay. Your friend saw the bones under the porch. Got the wrong idea. Shot me. Guess he thought I meant to kill you. Lord, I should have tried harder to scare you away. I'm sorry. I should have tried harder. Please... don't let me and your stupid, stupid friend die... in vain... please....

<u>THE STORM STOPS.</u>

<u>BIRDS BEGIN TO CHIRP AS THE SUN APPEARS.</u>

The world must be protected from this creature... they all have to be... it'll eat entire towns if you let it loose. (SHE NOTICES THE SUNRISE) oh, do you see that? The sunrise. I'll take it as a sign. And there's the rainbow. A promise of peace. Thank you. Thank you for taking over the house. Don't let anyone near it... thank you, thank you... (SHE DIES)

<u>MUSIC CUE:</u>
"THE MISTY LAKE"

VERONICA: Dash? Dash are you...? She's gone.

<u>THE HOUSE GROANS.</u>

And YOU. What are you? A demon house? And you can eat towns?

PORCH MOUTH: Eat... everything... eat.... eat.

VERONICA: I can relate. Wanting something so bad. Feeling that ache. Feels like the whole world destroyed you.

PORCH MOUTH: Destroyed...

VERONICA: You swallowed my friend.

He said he wanted to walk into these woods and be swallowed up. In a way... I guess he got his wish. But what about my wish? What about... yours? (BEAT) You've been deprived. Caged like a wild animal. I can see why you lash out. It's time you were free, don't ycu think?

PORCH MOUTH: To... eat?

VERONICA: Yes, but take me with you and I promise never to hold you back. We don't need any more of this... herb.

> VERONICA TOSSES THE HERB CANNISTER ASIDE.
>
> THE HOUSE DELIGHTFULLY GRUMBLES.

Let's find the nearest town. And the next one. And the next one. OH, THE PLACES WE WILL GO!

> MUSIC SWELLS.
>
> THE CABIN GRUMBLES IN VICTORY AND RISES FROM THE GROUND.
>
> IT STOMPS THROUGH THE FOREST.

END OF PLAY

Episode 4.9
AIN'T THE BIGGEST CITY
(Release date: September 14, 2023)

Written by Straton Rushing.

Originally written as a stage play but its world premiere was as an audio play on the Gather by the Ghost Light podcast before any stage productions.

Synopsis: When an inmate dies at the county jail under suspicious circumstances, the EMT who oversaw the affair is brought in for questioning. She might have a secret or two, but as connections arise more and more secrets arise to the surface.

<u>Audio Play Production</u>
Produced and directed by Jonathan Cook.
Cast: Arelis Rivera (Lane Hernandez); and Krys Bailey (Officer McAllen).
Music cues: "Outlawz" by WEARETHEGOOD.

Author (Straton Rushing) commentary: Growing up in rural west Texas, notions of "old west justice" are still prevalent in the culture I grew up in. The idea that true justice cannot always be reached through legal means was a sensibility I wanted to explore dramatically. The end result was "Ain't the Biggest City".

For licensing rights to this play, contact the playwright directly at StratonRushing@gmail.com.

SCRIPT: AIN'T THE BIGGEST CITY

CHARACTERS

LANE HERNANDEZ...   A Mexican-American woman in her 30s. She is an EMT for Val Verde County Hospital in Del Rio Texas

OFFICER MCALLEN...   A white man in his 40s originally from Del Rio. He is a police officer.

SETTING

An interrogation room in the Del Rio Police Department's station. Present Day.

	MUSIC CUE: "OUTLAWZ"
	LANE SITS ALONE IN THE ROOM. SHE SIGHS.
	HER CHAIR CREAKS AS SHE SHIFTS.
	DOOR OPENS AND CLOSES AS MCALLEN ENTERS.
MCALLEN:	Good morning Mrs... uhn.
	HE FLIPS PAPERS ON A CLIPBOARD AS HE SEARCHES FOR HER LAST NAME.

	I'm sorry.
LANE:	You can just call me Lane.
MCALLEN:	Lane. (BEAT) I'm Officer McAllen.
	<u>CHAIR CREAKS AS HE SITS IN A CHAIR ACROSS FROM HER.</u>
	Thank you for coming in this morning.
LANE:	I'm glad to help.
MCALLEN:	You're an EMT on the city ambulance?
LANE:	Yes.
MCALLEN:	How long you been doing that?
LANE:	About a year.
MCALLEN:	You're not originally from here, are you?
LANE:	No, we moved to Del Rio for this job. I'm from Odessa.
MCALLEN:	Had any trouble getting to know folks around here?
LANE:	Uhm I don't think so... I'm sorry but is that... pertinent to the investigation?
MCALLEN:	No. Not at all. It's just... Well, the other officers and I- we know most of the folks who work the ambulance. Obviously we see them when we respond to calls and well- when I asked about you, seemed like nobody knew who you were.
LANE:	(SHRUGS) I don't get out much outside of work. My son is

	four and, you know.
MCALLEN:	Keeps you pretty busy.
LANE:	He does indeed.
MCALLEN:	Alrighty Lane, I won't waste your time, I just have a few questions.

<u>FLIPS A PAGE ON HIS CLIPBOARD.</u>

Do you remember the call from last Thursday?

LANE:	The one here?
MCALLEN:	At the jail. The jail across the way. Yeah.
LANE:	Yep. Wouldn't be easy to forget that one.
MCALLEN:	Walk me thru it.
LANE:	Well, we got called to the jail. It was just me and one of the other EMTs. Ramirez... Have you talked to him already?
MCALLEN:	Yes ma'am, we talked to Jaime yesterday.
LANE:	Well, I guess you already know then. We got called to the jail around 3am 'cause an inmate had tried to hang himself. An officer who saw the inmate hanging suffered from a mild heart attack from the shock. Once we got there, Ramirez helped the officer. I went into the cell to tend to the inmate.
MCALLEN:	So you were in the cell alone with the inmate?

LANE: Briefly.

MCALLEN: Was that scary?

LANE: He was barely alive by the time we got there.

BEAT.

MCALLEN: Did you know the inmate?

LANE: Before I treated him?

MCALLEN: Yeah.

LANE: No. Why would I?

MCALLEN: Del Rio ain't the biggest city. I'd known him for years...

LANE: Well, I didn't know him personally. And I'm glad I didn't.

MCALLEN: Then I guess it's safe to say you knew of the inmate before?

LANE: ...guess so.

MCALLEN: How?

LANE: Jamie didn't tell you all this when you talked to him?

MCALLEN: I'd like to hear it from you Mrs. Hernandez.

LANE: Earlier you made it seem like you didn't know my name.

MCALLEN: What did you know about the inmate before you went in to save him?

LANE: I think his name was Leo. But Johnston was his last name, I think. A few days before he hung himself, we answered a call at his residence in the Lonestar trailer park. His

> girlfriend had called in saying she was worried about her son... Her 5-year-old had been staying with him while she was at work, so she wasn't there - but he was still inside when the officers arrived.

MUSIC CUE:
"OUTLAWZ"

MCALLEN: The officers arrived and arrested Johnston, then the ambulance was called-

LANE: To try to help the child. Of course, we just ended up taking him to the morgue.

MCALLEN: You were on that call, correct?

LANE: I was.

MCALLEN: So you know how Johnston killed the boy?

LANE: ...strangled him, with a bathroom towel.

MCALLEN: So it is safe to say you were very much aware of who Mr. Johnston was, and what he had done before you went into that cell to save his life... so what happened- did you give him CPR?

LANE: ...no.

MCALLEN: Wouldn't that have been standard procedure? He did still have a pulse-

LANE: Have you ever had to give CPR to someone?

MCALLEN: No ma'am.

LANE: I have more times than I can count. As soon as I saw Johnston I knew the only chance we had at saving him was by using a defibrillator. I focused on getting him into the ambulance to restart his heart that way.

MCALLEN FLIPS THROUGH PAGES ON HIS CLIPBOARD.

MCALLEN: Interesting that you mention that because the autopsy on Johnston's body seems to indicate he didn't receive any shocks from a defibrillator...

LANE: I drove the ambulance once we picked him up- I wasn't in the back. So I don't know what Jaime did to him after we loaded him up.

MCALLEN: You see this is where things get awfully blurry to me- Jaime's version of events say that you went into the jail cell to give him CPR. He also told me you said you failed to revitalize him-

LANE: Okay wait-

MCALLEN: Oddly enough Texas state law stipulates once CPR is commenced- the EMTs must continuously give it to the patient until they reach the hospital, and of course you know that... So why did you stop?

LANE: I'm leaving.

CHAIR CREAKS AS SHE STANDS.

<u>SHE WALKS TOWARD THE
DOOR.</u>

MCALLEN: No need for all of that Mrs. Hernandez- you aren't being charged with anything...

<u>SHE STOPS.</u>

Lane... Why do you think I called you in? (BEAT) Have you ever heard the saying "if a cop asks you something, it is because they already knew the answer"?

LANE: I think that saying applies more to a teenager hiding weed in their car than a real investigation.

MCALLEN: I know that you stood there and watched Leo Johnston die in that room right over there... every cell has a camera. We have the footage. First degree manslaughter at best. Every last bit of it on tape-

LANE: Were you on the Johnston call Officer McAllen?

MCALLEN: No.

LANE: I was the one who had to pick up that 5-year-old boy's body. I was the one who had to carry him. I was there...

MCALLEN: So... you'd like me to look the other way?

LANE: If you had half of a heart and an ounce of courage I think you'd have done the same thing I did. I don't know how you knew him before or who he was to you - I

don't' care. Johnston wanted
to die. Any sane person who
knew what he did would have
wanted him to die.

MCALLEN: Lane... there's something you
want from me ... You want me
to erase that tape. Think
about it- if I was some self-
riotous asshole who wanted to
ring you up on manslaughter
charges for allowing a baby-
killer to finish his
suicide... Why would I have
called you in to talk? Why
wouldn't I have just arrested
you? I already have all of
the evidence I need?

LANE: ...I don't know

MCALLEN: You're the loose end Lane...
Me, Jaime, every officer on
the Johnston call and
everyone else have our
stories straight. The problem
is, you are still the new kid
on the block-

LANE: I don't understand?

MCALLEN: The boy... You know his name
right?

LANE: They said it was Joshua.

MCALLEN: His murder case is still
open- we'll be turning over
all of the evidence to the DA
soon. But, before we do that-
we'd like to make sure every
EMT who was there agrees-
Joshua's mother was in the
house when the boy was
killed...

LANE: But she wasn't?

MCALLEN: You don't think so? Cause she
                  could have been... in fact
                  Ramirez and everyone else
                  agree she was actually there.
                  The police report says she
                  was there.

                        FLIPS THROUGH PAGES ON
                        HIS CLIPBOARD.

                  We even have testimony from a
                  neighbor that says she was
                  there... And if you happen to
                  agree with all of them...
                  then I figure we can have
                  that tape of you in the jail
                  cell erased.

LANE: Why do you want me to say she
                  was there?

MCALLEN: Helps- helps our case for the
                  charges we're about to press
                  on her. Accessory to Murder,
                  Neglect of a Child-

LANE: This woman just lost her son-
                  what are you hoping to gain
                  here?

MCALLEN: The same thing you were
                  looking for when you watched
                  Leo Johnston die... I'm
                  looking for that little bit
                  of justice. And if not that,
                  the next closes thing that I
                  can make happen.

LANE: She wasn't the one who killed
                  that boy.

MCALLEN: You can say she wasn't. But
                  she left him there- she knew
                  who Leo was - but let him
                  stay with him. He had a wrap
                  sheet. Used to beat his ex-
                  wife. Did you know that?

LANE: No-

MCALLEN: The child's grandmother
                didn't know where he was-
                none of us knew until Joshua
                turned up dead... Way I see
                it, she might have well have
                killed him herself. That is
                why I want to charge her...
                So... Do we have a deal?

LANE: You just admitted to me you
                are planning an illegal
                conspiracy to lock someone
                up-

MCALLEN: You might see it that way.
                But I just see it as
                strengthening a case to make
                sure things go the right way.

LANE: What's to stop me from
                telling the DA or someone
                higher up what's going on
                here-

MCALLEN: That's all fine and dandy if
                you want to do that Mrs.
                Hernandez... But deep down we
                both know you want to keep
                yourself out of trouble...
                you're not selling your soul
                to have the tape erased
                Lane... You're helping a good
                cause.

LANE: If you weren't on the initial
                Johnston call, why did they
                give the case to you now?

MCALLEN: The case isn't mine, not
                officially. I figured this
                went without saying, but this
                conversation isn't exactly an
                "official investigation" on
                the books.

LANE: But if everyone is in on

	this. Why are you the one talking to me?

<u>MCALLEN FLIPS THROUGH PAGES ON THE CLIPBOARD.</u>

MCALLEN:	You recognize that name on the report?
LANE:	Myra McAllen ... Your sister?

<u>MUSIC CUE: "OUTLAWZ"</u>

MCALLEN:	Sister-in-law... Former sister-in-law. She started dating Leo after my brother died.
LANE:	So that means Joshua was...
MCALLEN:	Yeah.
LANE:	I'm sorry...
MCALLEN:	Del Rio ain't that big. I never had any children of my own. So that kid meant the world to me... 'Specially after his dad passed... I tried to do what I could... You told me you have a son. So maybe, you'll have some idea where I am coming from... I wasn't there to save him... when he needed me the most... I should have been and I wasn't. One day I'm gonna see that little boy up in heaven and when I do I want him to know I did everything I could to make this right. He has to know someone cared, even if it was too late it still means something.
LANE:	So just like that?

MCALLEN: Do we have a deal?

<u>END OF PLAY</u>

Episode 4.10
SECONDHAND SOUL
(Release date: October 30, 2023)

Written by Ava Love Hanna.

Originally premiered as a stage play at Hyde Park Theatre[6] (Austin, TX) in April 2023 as part of Out of Ink: Family Traditions presented by ScriptWorks. The production was directed by Rosalind Faires.

Synopsis: Em and Vi are a couple in love who just moved into a new house. When Em attempts to use Vi's Ouija board to come out to her dead mother, she finds herself bargaining to save her soul from what she accidentally summons instead.

Audio Play Production
Produced and directed by Jonathan Cook.
Cast: Chelsea Glass (Em); Amy Thorne (Vi); and Evan Cook (Damon).
Music Cues: "Turtle Blues" by Ian Post; and "Lying to Myself" by Rue Knight.

Author (Ava Love Hanna) commentary: Secondhand Soul is one of my favorite plays, largely because of how it came together. Every November, I participate in two overlapping writing events: the Threshold Theatre Writing Challenge (30 daily prompts with strict deadlines) and the ScriptWorks Weekend Fling (a slightly longer than 24-hour playwriting competition with three required elements). One chaotic weekend a year, they overlap.

I wrote Secondhand Soul in about six hours on that fated weekend. Earlier in the month, Threshold had given us a prompt that read, "I may or may not have summoned a demon, but don't worry, he's friendly." And even though I didn't write anything based on it at the time, it sort of bounced around in my head and kept nagging at me because it felt exactly like the kind of thing that happens to me in my real life, "Hey, this insane thing is going on and I caused it, but don't worry, hopefully, it'll be funny."

Once the ScriptWorks Weekend Fling began and I was also up against the Threshold deadline, I knew I wanted to write the demon play and I wanted it to be a fun, chaotic comedy. I also wanted to play with the idea of keeping a secret about a character, not only from the other characters in the show, but from the audience as well. I wanted there to be a moment where everyone — on stage and off — realized what was going on at the same exact time. It's so much fun to watch the audience react to the reveal.

Beyond the comedy, Secondhand Soul is also a deeply personal play. It embodies the core themes of my work: strong women, queer joy, parental expectations, and the long winding road to acceptance. At its heart, it's inspired by my own experience of coming to terms with my sexuality while being raised in a conservative faith. Em's longing for her late mother's approval mirrors my own, while Vi is the version of myself I project to the world.

For licensing rights to this play, contact the playwright directly at avalovehanna@gmail.com.

SCRIPT: SECONDHAND SOUL

CHARACTERS

VI...	Playful, sarcastic, hates gym teachers.
EM...	Sweet, a little sheltered, madly in love with Vi.
DAMON...	Nice enough guy, but he

> really wants that soul.

<u>SETTING</u>

The living room of a small house in the midst of unpacking. Stormy night outside.

<u>FOOTSTEPS WALK AROUND
THE LIVING ROOM.</u>

<u>A THUNDERSTORM OUTSIDE.</u>

EM: What are you doing? Is that —

VI: Oh! Yeah, it's a Ouija board. I found it in my old stuff at my parent's house. You know, while I was there, I heard that our junior high gym teacher passed away... maybe we can use this to ask him what hell is like.

EM: No. Absolutely not. I don't want to mess with that stuff. Also, that's really mean, I liked him.

VI: You liked a gym teacher? What?? Gym teachers are our enemies. I... I feel like I don't even know you right now. The man wore tiny shorts and made us run around in circles for hours for literally no reason.

EM: Okay, his shorts were very short — probably unnecessarily so — but we didn't run for hours. We ran for thirty minutes. It was good for us!

VI: No. It was torture. In fact,

it's well known that running
was used as a type of
torture.

EM: They didn't torture people
with running - I'm gonna look
that up.

SHE GRABS HER PHONE.

Wait. No. We're getting off
track here. Please remove
your weird devil board from
our house. We just moved
here, and I don't want it
filled with ghosts and demons
and whatever else you conjure
up.

VI: (LAUGHS) Sit. Play with me.
It's a family tradition. My
sisters and I did this every
time we moved into a new
place. We'd explain to the
ghosts that we were very cool
people and ask them not to
watch us in the shower.

EM: I really don't want to mess
with this. My parents -

VI: - were weirdos who told you
everything was a sin. They
were wrong. You ready? Let's
do this!

EM: Yeah. (BEAT) I love our new
house. I want this to be a
happy place - which is why I
don't want you filling it
with ghosts - including the
ghosts of our past. Let the
gym teacher rest in peace.

VI: He was probably buried in
those shorts, you know. Don't
you want to ask him?

EM: No. Also, these things don't even work. How many dead people have you talked to?

VI: What?? They do work. This one was sold by the expert occultists at Hasbro. They wouldn't be able to sell something fake.

EM: That's not true. Companies sell fake stuff all the time. Dummies buy it anyway.

VI: When did your world view get so bleak? Everything is exactly as it says it is. Also, if Ouija boards are fake, then you can't be scared of it and you have to play with me. Okay, sit tight, I'm going to find some candles and snacks. We're gonna do this right.

<u>VI'S FOOTSTEPS EXIT.</u>

EM: This isn't scary. This is just a silly kid's toy. (PAUSES) It's weird though. Who looked at this and thought talking to dead people was a wholesome childhood activity? (BEAT) Alright. I'm gonna give this a shot.

<u>PLACES HER HANDS ON THE PLANCHETTE.</u>

(CLEARS THROAT) Hello? Spirits? Umm, if anyone is listening, this is Em.

<u>THUNDERSTRIKE.</u>

VI: (FROM OTHER ROOM) Whoa! Did you hear that? This is the

perfect weather to commune with the spirits!

EM: (CALLING OUT) Yeah. Are you coming back?

VI: (FROM OTHER ROOM) I think I've almost found the candle box. Aha! Nope, albums. False alarm. Oh! But I found my Dave Matthews record! Yes!

EM: No! I said nothing horrible in this house.

VI: (FROM OTHER ROOM) Heathen!

EM: (BACK TO THE OUIJA BOARD) Okay. For real this time.

PLACES HANDS ON THE PLANCHETTE.

Spirits. This is Em. (PAUSE) Hello? Can I ask for someone specific or do I leave a message?

THUNDERSTRIKE.

So, uh, I'd like to speak to my mom... I want to tell her I met someone, and she probably won't be happy about it, but that I'm happy and I love her. (PAUSE) Oh, wait, she's in conservative heaven and they've probably banned Ouija board messages there. So, I guess I'm happy speaking to anyone. Oh! But no demons. My parents warned me that demons are always first in line with these things and are just waiting to come get your soul. (LAUGHS TO HERSELF) That sounds so dumb when I say it out loud. But, uhh, just in case, I'm not interested in any demons today, please.

<u>THUNDERSTRIKE.</u>

<u>ELECTRICITY BUZZ AS LIGHTS FLICKER.</u>

Oh my God. Is that you? If there are spirits talking to me, please give me a sign — knock on something.

<u>HEAVY KNOCK ON THE FRONT DOOR.</u>

<u>EM IS STARTLED.</u>

<u>MUSIC CUE: "TURTLE BLUES"</u>

EM: Hello?

<u>MORE KNOCKING AT THE FRONT DOOR.</u>

<u>EM WALKS TO THE DOOR AND OPENS IT.</u>

Yes?

DAMON: Hi. You asked me to come?

EM: (PANICKED) What? I did?

DAMON: Yeah, you said just knock.

EM: Oh my god, I did. Who are you?

DAMON: I'm Damon.

EM: Demon??

DAMON: (CONFUSED) I guess that's one way to say it. I prefer Damon though. DAY-MON.

EM: Oh my God, Oh my God, Oh my God.

DAMON: So, uh, I came about the

	soul? Can I come in? It's really pouring out here.
EM:	Soul??

<u>DAMON'S FOOTSTEPS ENTER.</u>

<u>EM CLOSES THE DOOR.</u>

DAMON:	I love the rainy weather, but I hate getting wet. It feels so gross.
EM:	I'm sure you're used to warmer climes.
DAMON:	I am! How did you know that?
EM:	Oh, I know too much stuff. Okay, listen, I think there's been a mistake. (TO HERSELF) I can't believe my parents were right.
DAMON:	Are you saying you've changed your mind about the soul? Aww, please don't do that. I came all this way. I was really looking forward to bringing it home today.
EM:	I feel bad, I do, but I just don't think I want to part with it. I need it. Also, my girlfriend will be really mad. I did this without her.
DAMON:	Ohhh, I get it. Listen, let's do this — I can wait until the storm passes and then we can take a look at the soul, see what kind of condition it's in, you can talk to your girlfriend about it, and then we can make a deal. Okay?

<u>VI ENTERS SINGING TO HERSELF.</u>

VI: (TO DAMON) Oh! Hi! I didn't know we were expecting anyone.

DAMON: Yeah, I came by—

EM: —to welcome us to the neighborhood! (PLEADING) Right, Damon?

DAMON: Yeah... sure... that's something I'd like to do. You have a lovely home.

VI: Well, thanks! Sorry, everything's a mess, we're still unpacking. Please have a seat. I'm 90% certain there's a couch in this room, but really, anything can be a seat if you try hard enough.

DAMON BEGINS FIDDLING WITH HIS COAT.

DAMON: No worries. Is it okay if I take off this wet coat? I'm not used to this weather. I'm more of a dry heat kind of guy.

VI: Of course! Em, will you take his coat to the kitchen? There's towels in there.

EM: (SNAPPING OUT OF IT) Oh! Um, okay, sure. I'll just take this nice normal person's coat to the kitchen in our house. I can do that.

VI: Okay... good? (TO DAMON) Sorry she's being weird. I found my old Ouija board and she's pretty skittish about that kind of stuff.

DAMON: Ha. I always wanted to play with one of those! My parents

	wouldn't buy one.
VI:	Said you'd summon demons?
DAMON:	No. Said it was fake.
VI:	Monsters.
DAMON:	Exactly.
VI:	So, what do you do for a living Damon?
DAMON:	I'm a fitness instructor.
VI:	(SUSPICIOUS) A fitness instructor? As in... at a gym? Like a gym teacher? Where people run? Do you make people run, Damon?
DAMON:	Uh, sorta? I encourage people to run, yes.
VI:	(COLDLY) I see.
DAMON:	Exercise is good, right? Tearing muscle fibers, growing new ones. Tearing people apart and rebuilding them is my whole job.

<u>EM ENTERS, HEARING DAMON'S LINE OUT OF CONTEXT.</u>

EM:	Oh my god!
VI:	It's torture!
DAMON:	(LAUGHS) That's one way to look at it. Is it okay if I use your restroom?
EM:	Sure. It's right through that hallway, second door on the left.

<u>DAMON EXITS.</u>

VI:	Em, that guy is evil. He seems so nice, but he's the

	worst kind of person and he's here in our home. Our home! I, I don't understand how this happened.
EM:	Yeah, I know. I'm so sorry, I wanted to tell you, but –

<u>DAMON ENTERS.</u>

DAMON:	Thanks. Just needed to wash my hands. You would not believe the stuff that gets on my hands at work.
EM:	(WEAKLY) Uh huh. I can imagine. Oh wow, my throat is really dry. Vi, can you get us all some water, please?
VI:	Sure. Ice?
DAMON:	None for me.
EM:	(TO DAMON) Of course not. (TO VI) Room temp is fine.
VI:	Okay, one cold, delicious water for me, and two room temperature waters for weirdos coming right up.

<u>VI EXITS.</u>

<u>MUSIC CUE:</u>
<u>"TURTLE BLUES"</u>

DAMON:	So, about that soul. Can I at least look at it? Make sure it's in good shape?
EM:	What?? No. That's weird!
DAMON:	I just want to make sure it's in good condition. You should see what some people do to their souls. I mean, they can take a lot of abuse, but still.

EM: I assure you, mine is fine. Pristine even. You'd be lucky to have it! (RECONSIDERS) I mean... um, no. You don't want this old thing. It's all old and used.

DAMON: Oh, used souls are great! They last forever, you know. Oh sure, some people prefer new, but I prefer older ones. They have more character. And, I don't have the stress of having to break them in.

EM: Break them in??

VI ENTERS.

VI: Break what in?

EM: (HYSTERICAL) Babies! I think he's talking about babies!

VI: What? You're making babies run now?? That's too far! (TO EM) I told you this guy is the worst!

VI SPILLS THE WATER ON DAMON.

Oh! Sorry about that. The glass slipped out of my hand.

DAMON: Um, no worries. I'll just go dry off again.

DAMON EXITS.

VI: That man is evil.

EM: (PACNICKED RAMBLING) I know! Look, I need to tell you something. I think I've ruined our lives and I really don't want you to be mad at me, especially because I'm probably about to go to hell, but while you were getting

	snacks – which you were doing because you're so thoughtful and I love that about you – I love everything about you – I've always loved you since the moment I first saw you in our junior high gym class but my parents said I couldn't go to heaven if I kissed girls so I never said anything back then – but I played with the Ouija board by myself to try to tell my mom about us and I think I summoned a demon on accident and I'm soooooo sorry.
VI:	You've loved me since junior high gym class?
EM:	Yeah. That's why I didn't mind the running. Or the gym teacher. It was the one place I knew I would get to see you every day.
VI:	That is really sweet.
EM:	It doesn't matter now though because he's here for my soul.

<u>DAMON ENTERS.</u>

DAMON:	Oh, good you told her! Yeah, I'm here to buy the soul. Can we make a deal?
EM:	I told you I need it! I have too much to live for! It's not for sale!
VI:	Wait. You're here to buy the soul? What day is it?
EM:	It's Saturday, the 5th. Why?
VI:	Ohhhh! (TO DAMON) I'm so sorry! I thought we were

meeting next week on the 12th!

EM: What?? You planned this! You were going to sell MY soul to a demon next week?

DAMON: It's pronounced Day-mon. Daaaaay-mon.

VI: Em, no. I'm selling my old Kia Soul. This must be the guy I've been texting with about it.

<u>MUSIC CUE:
"LYING TO MYSELF"</u>

DAMON: That's me! The soul guy.

EM: (RELIEVED) Oh! Ohhhhh. Oh my God. So, I didn't summon a demon then? That is such a relief. So, this guy isn't evil then?

VI: Oh, he's still evil – he's a gym teacher.

DAMON: Hey!

VI: But... it seems like maybe I've been wrong. I owe a lot to gym class.

DAMON: See? Running is good for you!

VI: No! Get out, vile demon!

<u>VI SHOVES DAMON OUT THE
FRONT DOOR.</u>

<u>END OF PLAY</u>

Episode 4.11 & 4.12
KINGDUMB
(Release date: November 13, 2023)

Written by Jonathan Cook.

Originally produced as a live audio play recording for the Gather by the Ghost Light podcast. The live event took place on October 21, 2023 at Le Chat Noir[9] in Augusta, GA. The live recording was released as a two-part episode.

Synopsis: There's a new King in the land that has initiated a mysterious new tax on the citizens. Outraged, the region's finest Clock fixer, aka "Time Repair Specialist", recruits some of the most unlikely rebels to help him develop a plan to overthrow the King. Their plotting takes them on a comedic journey through perilous mountain tops all the way to the palace itself where they confront this vile King face to face. Medieval fantasy comedy.

<u>Live Audio Play Production</u>
Produced and directed by Jonathan Cook.
Foley effects by TJ McSherry.
Cast: Julian Diaz (Corbin); Marian Thibodeau (Cayly); Luke Romagnoli (Oswaldo); Devon McSherry (Henry Hackus); Arelis Rivera (Estelle Avery); Adam Cowart (D. Duncan); Robb Smith (Deke Harvey); Michael Silvio Fortino (King Amado); Krys Bailey

(Leon); Brandon Dawson (Richard Taxman); Chelsea Glass (Guard Herman); Jonathan Cook (Guard Bellywax and Narrator); Eric Odom (Jeremy the Sage); and Karla Fischbach (Lenny the Dragon Slayer).

Author (Jonathan Cook) commentary: This live audio production was an amazing feat and our first live show for Gather by the Ghost Light. "Kingdumb" is a play that I wrote about a decade ago — my first full-length play. It's silly. It's absurd. And it's so dang funny. At least I always thought so. Its comedic style is a bit of Mel Brooks mixed with Terry Pratchett and at the time that I wrote it, my more popular plays that were tending to get a lot of traction and being produced all over the place were a different brand. Darker. More Twilight Zone-ish. So at the time, "Kingdumb" didn't really feel like the voice I was going for as a playwright and it ultimately went into my vault of unproduced works.

That was until we started throwing around the idea of recording an audio play live on stage in front of an audience. I always felt a full-length comedy would work best for this kind of thing. And it seemed like this would be the perfect time to give "Kingdumb" a home and let people experience the story.

And the live show SOLD OUT. Not an empty seat in the house. It went over better than I ever imagined and the audience loved the story and especially the characters that were brought to life by our marvelous actors.

PUBLISHER NOTE: "Kingdumb" by Jonathan Cook is a full-length play that was recorded as a live event. With that in mind, we unfortunately couldn't fit the script for a full-length play in this anthology, but the full script is available at Ghost Light Publications (ghostlightpubs.com).

For licensing rights to this play, please contact info@ghostlightpubs.com.

Episode 4.13
SANTA THE CLAUSE
(Release date: December 4, 2023)

Written by Ron Burch.

Originally produced as a stage play at Playground LA[10] at the Zephyr Theatre, Los Angeles, CA, on December 8, 2014. Directed by Sylvia Blush.

Synopsis: Santa Claus and his elf Beedle visit the holiday office party of Mr. Hargraves, the rich CEO of Awesome Toys, to make him an offer he can't refuse.

<u>Audio Play Production</u>
Produced and directed by Jonathan Cook.
Cast: Robb Smith (Santa Claus); Everette Street (Mr. Hargraves); and Kayla Gardner (Beedle the Elf).
Music Cues: "Christmas Day" by Foster; and "Dance of the Sugar Plum Fairy" by Ian Post.

Author (Ron Burch) commentary: Santa don't play.

For licensing rights to this play, contact the playwright directly at burchre@gmail.com.

SCRIPT: <u>SANTA THE CLAUSE</u>

<u>CHARACTERS</u>

HARGRAVES...	Male, Age 40 – 45, Any race, CEO of "Awesome Toys"
BEEDLE...	Female, Age 25 – 30, Any race, Elf
SANTA CLAUS...	Male, Age 50-55 (but ageless), Any race

<u>SETTING</u>

The office holiday party of Mr. Hargraves. Night.

	<u>MUSIC CUE: "CHRISTMAS DAY"</u>
	<u>IN THE OFFICE OF HARGRAVES.</u>
	<u>A COMPANY CHRISTMAS PARTY IS HEARD RIGHT OUTSIDE THE DOOR – PEOPLE CHATTING, MUSIC, ETC.</u>
HARGRAVES:	I'm sorry, I'm just stunned. I mean, Santa lands his sleigh on our helicopter pad with his elf and he wants to talk to me? I'm blown away. Where is he?
BEEDLE:	He's coming. He doesn't want to make a big deal of it.
	<u>SANTA MAKES A MAGICAL ENTRANCE.</u>

SANTA: Merry Christmas! Ho, ho, ho!

HARGRAVES: Wow, I can't believe it. You are actually Santa Clause. I mean, I didn't think you actually existed. But the sleigh and the reindeer and it's like a childhood dream come true. It's so great to meet you.

SANTA: Thank you, Mr. Hargraves. I hope we're not causing too much trouble by dropping by your office holiday party.

HARGRAVES: Not at all, Santa, not at all. Do you think I could let my employees meet you?

SANTA: You know, it's better in these situations to let them have their fun.

HARGRAVES: Oh, you mean not to give away that you exist.

MUSIC CUE:
"DANCE OF THE SUGAR
PLUM FAIRY"

SANTA: Mmm, not actually. (NO LONGER MERRY; MORE GANGSTER) Sit the fuck down.

HARGRAVES: Huh?

BEEDLE: He said SIT.

BEEDLE PUSHES HARGRAVES
INTO HIS CHAIR.

HARGRAVES: Hey! What's going on?

SANTA: Shut up, Hargraves.

HARGRAVES: Excuse me?

SANTA: Don't try to soft soap me with all that nostalgic

	sentimental bullshit. You know why I'm here.
HARGRAVES:	To spread holiday cheer?
SANTA:	Fuck holiday cheer.
HARGRAVES:	I don't understand.
	<u>HARGRAVES TRIES TO STAND, BUT BEEDLE PUSHES HIM BACK DOWN.</u>
BEEDLE:	Don't move.
SANTA:	I wouldn't mess with Beedle.
HARGRAVES:	Your elf? Be serious.
BEEDLE:	Don't make me fuck you up.
	<u>BEEDLE PUSHES HIM.</u>
HARGRAVES:	Hey!
SANTA:	Listen, Hargraves, I know who you are. You're the CEO of Awesome Toys. Right now your company is the most profitable toy company in the world.
HARGRAVES:	So?
SANTA:	I want my cut.
HARGRAVES:	Your cut of what?
SANTA:	My profit.
HARGRAVES:	What're you talking about?!
BEEDLE:	(MENACINGLY) You call him "Mr. Clause."
HARGRAVES:	Sorry. What are you talking about, Mr. Clause?
SANTA:	For years, I busted my ass bringing free toys to all the boys and girls. Out of the goodness of my heart for kids who had hard lives. But then

you corporations stepped in. You use my name. You force all the parents into buying tons of your expensive toys under the guise that "Santa" is bringing them.

HARGRAVES: So?

SANTA: You come into my territory and make money off my back.

HARGRAVES: Well, I wouldn't put it that way.

SANTA: Beedle, would you put it that way?

BEEDLE: I definitely would, Mr. Clause.

HARGRAVES: I'm sure we can come to some understanding.

SANTA: You're goddamn right we're coming to an understanding. Pay me or you'll find your feet in cement booties.

BEEDLE: Love cement booties.

SANTA: You toy companies have pimped my name enough. I want my percentage.

HARGRAVES: And what if I don't?

SANTA: Beedle takes you for a sleigh ride.

BEEDLE: (CHUCKLES) Oh fun!

HARGRAVES: Is this some kind of joke?

<u>SANTA WALKS OVER TO HARGRAVES AND GRABS HIM.</u>

SANTA: (DEADLY SERIOUS) Are you saying I'm not really Santa Clause, punk?

HARGRAVES: Well...

SANTA: You know how tired I am of that? How would you like to have thousands of people dress up like you, say they're you and get away with all kinds of shit. Make money off your image and there's very little you can do about it 'cause you're supposed to be fucking jolly.

HARGRAVES: Guess I'd be annoyed.

SANTA: Ho fucking ho you would be.

HARGRAVES: (TRYING TO LIGHTEN THE SITUATION) So I guess I'm kinda on your Naughty list.

SANTA: If you were on my Naughty list, the next time someone saw you, it'd be in pieces.

BEEDLE: I'm good with a saw.

<u>SANTA TAKES OUT A PIECE OF PAPER.</u>

SANTA: Here's our contract. Sign it.

HARGRAVES: I can't really sign anything until the company lawyers take a look at it --

SANTA: Beedle, the nutcracker.

<u>BEEDLE STARTS CLAMPING AWAY ON A GRINDING ELECTRONIC NUTCRACKER AS SHE HUMS ALONG TO "DANCE OF THE SUGAR PLUM FAIRY".</u>

HARGRAVES: Whoa, whoa, whoa.

SANTA: You whoa. I'm tired of whoaing. You don't sign this contract, Beedle's gonna squeeze your nuts into "nuthingness." And what? You call the cops and tell them Santa and his elf roughed you up?

<u>BEEDLE LAUGHS.</u>

No one's gonna believe that. Know why? 'Cause I'm a fuckin' myth. They'll put you in the loony bin, you and your compressed nuts.

HARGRAVES:	You're serious about this --
SANTA:	How big is your house?
HARGRAVES:	I don't see what business --
SANTA:	Beedle, nutcracker.

<u>BEEDLE TURNS ON THE NUTCRACKER AGAIN AND ONCE AGAIN HUMS ALONG TO "DANCE OF THE SUGAR PLUM FAIRY."</u>

HARGRAVES:	Over 6000 square feet!
SANTA:	How many acres you own?
HARGRAVES:	Over ten.
SANTA:	And that includes?

<u>HARGRAVES HESITATES.</u>

BEEDLE:	Can I feed him to the reindeer, Mr. Clause?
HARGRAVES:	A pool, tennis courts, basketball court, and a separate movie theatre.
SANTA:	You have your own movie theatre.
HARGRAVES:	It only seats 40.
SANTA:	You know where I live?

HARGRAVES: The North Pole.

SANTA: (MAKES A BUZZER NOISE) Cleveland. Couldn't afford the Pole anymore. You know what it costs to feed reindeer and elves? A shitload of money, that's what. Especially when you work freelance like I do. I haven't had a new suit in over 100 years.

BEEDLE: I miss the Pole.

SANTA: We all do, Beedle, we all do. But with the help of Mr. Hargraves here and all the other toy company CEOs, we're going to be back on top soon.

HARGRAVES: Maybe you need to go into a different line of work?

SANTA: A different line of work. I'm Santa, cocksucker. I am Christmas. I am Christmas Spirit and Christmas Joy and all that other jolly shit. Now sign.

       SANTA SLAMS THE CONTRACT DOWN ON THE DESK.

HARGRAVES: (THINKING QUICKLY) What if I hired you?

SANTA: And what if I was the Tooth Fairy.

BEEDLE: (LASCIVIOUS) I love the Tooth Fairy.

HARGRAVES: I'm serious. I'll give you your own toy line. What do you think about that?

SANTA: Keep talking.

HARGRAVES: We'll call it "Santa's Brand." Supervised by "The Clause" himself. We'll split the profit ... fifty-fifty.

BEEDLE: Be better if Santa was getting 75.

HARGRAVES: Okay, 75.

SANTA: I bring my elves with me?

HARGRAVES: You got it.

SANTA: I call the shots.

HARGRAVES: Whatever you want.

SANTA: What's the catch?

HARGRAVES: I'm the only toy company you go with.

SANTA: And why should I agree to this?

HARGRAVES: Steady job. Benefits. Health. 401K.

BEEDLE: Does that include dental?

HARGRAVES: Sure does. Ask all my happy workers out there.

BEEDLE: Santa, I really need dental. Ever since Rudolph kicked me in the head.

SANTA: But I get to call my own shots.

HARGRAVES: If I get "Santa," whatever you want.

SANTA: Okay, deal. (THEY SHAKE) But don't make me go Krampus on your ass.

HARGRAVES: I'll get my lawyers right now and have them start drawing up the contracts.

HARGRAVES EXCITEDLY
EXITS.

BEEDLE: Santa, I just don't understand why you want to be in business with that person.

SANTA: Because, as I was hoping, Beedle, I get to "call the shots."

BEEDLE: What does that mean?

SANTA: Get my holiday back. And provide free toys for the kids again. As Mr. Hargraves will eventually find out.

BEEDLE: Ahhhh, that's why you're Santa.

SANTA: When you're dealing with business people, you gotta talk their language. "Fuckin' B."

BEEDLE: Uh, that's "Fuckin' A," Santa.

SANTA: Sorry, I'll get it right eventually. (BACK TO THE OLD SANTA WE ALL KNOW AND LOVE) Ho, ho, ho, Merry Christmas!

JOLLY JINGLE CLOSER.

END OF PLAY

Episode 4.14
SANTA DOESN'T LIVE HERE ANYMORE
(Release date: December 18, 2023)

Written by Patrick Gabridge.

Originally premiered as a stage play at the Phoenix Theatre[11] in Indianapolis, IN on November 28, 2014, as part of "A Very Phoenix XMas 9: Flashing Through the Snow Festival. Original cast: Lincoln Slentz (Jeffrey); Dave Ruark (Dad); and Carly Kincannon (Mom). It was directed by Bryan Fonseca.

Synopsis: Mom and Dad have never gotten around to telling Jeffrey that there's no Santa. He's 30, and he still believes. This Christmas the truth comes out about Santa, as well as a few other family secrets.

<u>Audio Play Production</u>
Produced and directed by Jonathan Cook.
Cast: Marian Thibodeau (Mom); Krys Bailey (Dad); and Michael Silvio Fortino (Jeffrey).
Music Cues: "The Red and Green" by Ty Simon: and "Santa's New Suit" by Southside Aces.

Author (Patrick Gabridge) commentary: I was a kid who believed about Santa until he was older than most, and one of my own kids was the same--so I get Jeffrey, completely. I've had the good fortune to see this play performed by many companies, across the country (it's also had productions and readings in France, Canada, Argentina, and South Korea), and we always have a good time with it. But there's a whole area of darkness underlying this play, and any production has to tread a delicate balance between the light and dark, truth and lies. Which helps it all play out for a fun time for the audience.

For licensing rights to this play, contact the playwright directly at pat@gabridge.com.

SCRIPT: SANTA DOESN'T LIVE HERE ANYMORE

CHARACTERS

DAD...   Dad.

MOM...   Mom.

JEFFREY...   Their son. About 30.

SETTING

Christmas Eve.
A living room.

A FIREPLACE CRACKLES.

MOM IS WRAPPING PRESENTS AS SHE HUMS TO HERSELF.

DAD: Better do my duty.

DAD MUNCHES ON COOKIES.

MOM: That's a lot of cookies.

DAD: Santa has a powerful appetite.

MOM: And a belly like a bowl full of jelly.

DAD: Full of cookies.

MOM: Seriously.

DAD: Where's your Christmas
                spirit?

MOM: Mine? You're the one who
                thinks we should--

DAD: But here we are. You win.

MOM: And you get cookies.

                JEFFREY ENTERS WITH A
                BIG YAWN.

JEFFREY: Dad! What are you doing?

                PUTS COOKIES BACK ON
                THE PLATE.

DAD: (MOUTHFUL OF COOKIES)
                Nothing. Just, ah--

JEFFREY: And Mom. Why are you messing
                with my stocking?

MOM: I, well, I was...

JEFFREY: Did Santa come early?

MOM: Exactly. You just missed him.

JEFFREY: Oh, wow.

MOM: And he was so generous. Look
                at all these great presents.
                And he even said your father
                could have his cookies.

JEFFREY: That's so... hard to...

DAD: Believe?

JEFFREY: They're really good cookies.

MOM: So, why don't you go back to
                bed, dear? I was just going
                to hang this up.

JEFFREY: I won't be able to sleep now.
                Can't I just see what he gave
                me?

MOM: Tomorrow.

JEFFREY: Please?

MOM: You heard me.

JEFFREY: Okay. Good night. Merry Christmas.

MOM: Merry Christmas, Jeffrey.

<u>JEFFREY EXITS.</u>

DAD: This is insane.

MOM: I think it's sweet.

DAD: He's thirty years old and still believes in Santa.

MOM: We said we'd let him figure it out on his own.

DAD: For most kids that doesn't get them past age 12.

MOM: It's not hurting anything.

DAD: I blame myself. Those early years of making little ashy footprints around the fireplace, and reindeer tracks on the lawn and the notes and the letters and the cookies and half-drunk glasses of milk.

MOM: It was all for fun. And love. Isn't that what it is? A great big symbol of unbridled generosity and love. What's wrong with believing in that?

DAD: Because it's a symbol. It's not real. At some point there comes a time when...

<u>MUSIC CUE:</u>
<u>"THE RED AND GREEN"</u>

I mean, what about this

	Peterson girl he's dating, does she know that he still believes in--

<u>JEFFREY ENTERS.</u>

JEFFREY:	Still believes in what?
MOM:	Nothing, honey. You should get some sleep.
JEFFREY:	You know, I've been wondering...
DAD:	Yes?
JEFFREY:	Well... Nothing.
DAD:	Go ahead and ask. We'll answer.
JEFFREY:	No, that's okay. I'll just go back to bed.

<u>JEFFREY STARTS TO EXIT.</u>

DAD:	There's no Santa.
MOM:	You are a very bad man.
DAD:	It's been me and Mom, this whole time.
JEFFREY:	That's impossible.
MOM:	We agreed to wait.
DAD:	He was never going to ask.
JEFFREY:	Seriously? Where's your workshop? You're here, right now. If you were Santa, you'd be out delivering presents all around the world.
DAD:	No. It's... The other parents are in on it, too. They all do it for their own kids. See?
JEFFREY:	You mean there is a gigantic worldwide conspiracy where

	hundreds of millions of parents conspire to dupe their children into thinking there's a magic elf who delivers gifts? They buy extra presents, put up stockings, and tell stories about the North Pole and reindeer. All carefully aligned. Under whose coordination?
DAD:	Coordination?
JEFFREY:	You're telling me that an effort like this just happens, that somehow everyone knows how and when to do this?
DAD:	Pretty much, yeah.
JEFFREY:	How is that even possible? The scope of it is just... mindboggling. I don't... Next you'll say that the Easter Bunny--
DAD:	Same deal.
MOM:	What are you doing?
DAD:	Let's get it all out.
JEFFREY:	Is it every holiday? Thanksgiving?
DAD:	The pilgrims didn't do so great by the Indians.
MOM:	Native Americans.
DAD:	It was the start of a massive genocide, actually. Started with Columbus.
JEFFREY:	Not Columbus Day. Christopher Columbus sailed the ocean blue.

DAD: And killed a couple million Arawaks on the island of Haiti. All of them, actually.

MOM: I want a divorce.

DAD: And our real last name is Steinberg, not Smith. Racial redlining was invented by the government. Bush did not defeat Al Gore. JFK cheated on his wife. The NSA listens to our phone conversations. Supermodels have pores in their skin. Dumbledore is gay and also fictional.

MOM: Mr. Peterson is your real father.

DAD: (TOGETHER) What?
JEFFREY: (TOGETHER What!?

MOM: So you really should not be dating Jane.

JEFFREY: Oh.

MOM: (TO DAD) And you know how much you like that deli scene from When Harry Met Sally?

DAD: Come on.

MOM: I'm a much better actress than Meg Ryan.

DAD: That can't be true.

MOM: You seemed so proud of yourself. And those spa weekends I said I spent with my sister?

DAD: Were like the fishing trips I supposedly took with Jerry?

MOM: Oh.

JEFFREY: I can't believe you lied to

me. For so long.

DAD: Seems like we have a talent
            for it.

MOM: We just wanted you to be
            happy.

DAD: It's a cold, miserable world
            out there, buddy.

MOM: And we wanted to protect you
            from it. As long as we could.

JEFFREY: Supermodels really have
            pores?

DAD: Just like the rest of us.

JEFFREY: And racial segregation...

DAD: Didn't just happen all by
            itself.

JEFFREY: And the tooth fairy?

DAD: Mom has a whole bag of your
            baby teeth.

JEFFREY: Ewww.

MOM: What am I supposed to do?
            Throw them in the trash?

JEFFREY: I'm not sure what's real
            anymore.

DAD: Me neither. (TO MOM) You
            really want a divorce?

JEFFREY: I'll be from a broken home.
            With no Santa.

MOM: I don't know.

JEFFREY: Can't we just go back to how
            things were?

DAD: I'll try harder. Whatever it
            takes.

MOM: Really?

JEFFREY:	Hello. We're talking about Santa here.
DAD:	You are. We're not.
JEFFREY:	I'm having an existential crisis.
MOM:	Honey, you need to get a job, move out, and stop believing in Santa Claus.
JEFFREY:	But. But. Mom?
MOM:	Jeffrey, Jeffrey, Jeffrey. What took you so long to even wonder?
JEFFREY:	I love the magic of Christmas morning. The way the entire world glows with love and possibility. I want that feeling to last every second of every day. What kind of person wants to poke their fingers through that shiny scene to touch the dark and dirty parts behind it?
MOM:	Someone has to pay the price for all those things you choose not to see.
JEFFREY:	I don't care. I want the magic.
DAD:	We all do.
JEFFREY:	How about just on Christmas? We can go back to... tomorrow morning, let's just act like nothing ever happened. Okay? One more time?
DAD:	I don't know.
MOM:	I suppose it wouldn't hurt.
DAD:	(TO MOM) Well. If that works for you.

MOM:	It might. I don't know.
DAD:	But the rest of it--
JEFFREY:	Message received. Loud and clear. Job, apartment, dump Jane. But tomorrow morning?
DAD:	Okay.
MOM:	Really?
JEFFREY:	Thanks! And next year, I'll do the stockings. For both of you. It's like I'll actually become Santa. Crazy! Good night!
	HE HUGS THEM BOTH THEN EXITS.
MOM:	Good night, dear.
DAD:	Well. Merry Christmas.
	CLOSING MUSIC: "SANTA'S NEW SUIT"

END OF PLAY

Episode 4.15
IMMERSION THERAPY
(Release date: January 16, 2024)

Written by David MacGregor.

Originally premiered as a stage play at Tipping Point Theatre[12] (Northville, MI) in June 2014 as part of their Sandbox Play Festival. Synopsis: The best husband in the world gives his wife the ultimate birthday present.

<u>Audio Play Production</u>
Produced and directed by Jonathan Cook.
Cast: Devon McSherry (Melissa); Jonathan Cook (Doug): and Tommy Cooper (Droppo the Clown).
Music Cues: "Little Duke" by Southside Aces.

Author (David MacGregor) commentary: Once upon a time, when I was a young lad, my loving parents took me to the Thanksgiving Parade in Detroit, Michigan. There we stood on the curb of Woodward Avenue, watching the bands and floats go by, waiting in heightened expectation for the arrival of Santa...and just as I caught a glimpse of jolly old St. Nick, a clown stuck his face three inches from mine and growled, "Merry Christmas, little man!" The play is fiction. The trauma is not. Enjoy!

For licensing rights to this play, contact the playwright directly at dmacgregor77@gmail.com.

SCRIPT: IMMERSION THERAPY

CHARACTERS

DOUG...   A man in his late 20s-40s.

MELISSA...   A woman in her late 20s-40s.

DROPPO...   A clown of indeterminate age.

SETTING

A living room.
The present.

	MUSIC CUE: "LITTLE DUKE"
	MELISSA FLIPS THROUGH TRAVEL MAGAZINES.
	CAR PULLS UP OUTSIDE.
	CAR DOOR OPENS AND CLOSES.
MELISSA:	Finally he's home! Can't wait to see what he has in store this year! Hi hon!
DOUG:	There she is!
	DOUG KISSES HER.
	Happy Birthday, sweetheart! How's your day been so far?
MELISSA:	It's been okay. Nothing special... yet. (WAITING) Well...?
DOUG:	Well what?

MELISSA: You'd better be kidding.

DOUG: About what?

MELISSA: Oh my God. Don't do this to me.

DOUG: I'm not sure I follow you.

MELISSA: My present? An amazing, one-of-a-kind, incredible birthday present!

DOUG: Oh... that's right. I usually try to get you a little something for your birthday, don't I?

MELISSA: A little something? A signed first edition of Ulysses by James Joyce? Skydiving over the Mojave Desert at sunset? Dinner at The French Laundry? Honey, your presents... my girlfriends want to slit my throat when they hear what you get me for my birthday.

DOUG: Well, birthdays are special. They should be special.

MELISSA: So what is it this year? Can I guess?

DOUG: Now honey, you know that every year it gets harder and harder to do something amazing, right?

MELISSA: Not for you.

DOUG: Well, I do my best, but I just want you to know that if I'm going to keep up the standards, I need to start thinking more and more outside the box.

MELISSA: Oh my God... it's going to be... just tell me, is it a

	present or an experience?
DOUG:	Kind of both... maybe leaning a little more to the experience side.
MELISSA:	Really? Do I need to pack? Where are we going?
DOUG:	For this experience, you just need to stand right there.
MELISSA:	Right here?
DOUG:	Right there. And close your eyes.

<u>MELISSA WITH A BIG
FRUSTRATED SIGH.</u>

Ah, ah, ah, close 'em.

<u>SHE CLOSES HER EYES.</u>

MELISSA:	Okay, they're closed. Bring it on.

<u>DOUG MOVES TOWARDS THE
DOOR.</u>

Oh my God... oh my God... how long do I have to wait?

DOUG:	Not long. Just keep your eyes closed.

<u>DOUG OPENS THE FRONT
DOOR.</u>

<u>DROPPO ENTERS. HIS
CLOWN SHOES SQUEAK AS
HE WALKS.</u>

(WHISPERING) Come on in. Over here.

DROPPO:	Over there?
DOUG:	Yeah. Go stand right in front of her.
MELISSA:	Still waiting!

<u>DROPPO SQUEAKS OVER TO
MELISSA.</u>

DOUG: Are you ready?

MELISSA: Yes!

DOUG: Open your eyes!

<u>MELISSA OPENS HER EYES.</u>

DROPPO: HAPPY BIRTHDAY!!!

<u>DROPPO HONKS A HORN.</u>

<u>THEN HE SINGS "HAPPY
BIRTHDAY" TO THE TURN
OF "THE WILLIAM TELL
OVERTURE".</u>

<u>HIS FEET ARE DANCING
THE WHOLE TIME.</u>

Happy happy birthday!
Happy happy birthday!
Happy happy birthday!
Happy happy birthday!
Happy Happy Happy Happy Happy
Happy Birthday!
Happy Happy Happy Happy Happy
Happy Birthday!
Happy Happy Birthday!
Happy Happy Birthday!
Happy Happy Birthday!
Happy Happy Birthday!

<u>DROPPO DROPS HIS HORN
TOWARDS THE END OF THE
SONG.</u>

<u>BUT QUICKLY PICKS IT UP
AND GIVES IT A GOOD
HONK.</u>

<u>MELISSA SCREAMS FOR ALL
SHE'S WORTH. TERRIFIED.
SHE CONTINUES TO
WHIMPER THROUGHOUT THE
FOLLOWING DIALOGUE.</u>

DROPPO: I don't think your wife likes clowns.

DOUG: No. Actually, she's terrified of clowns. Has been as long as I've known her. It's not that uncommon apparently. It's called coulrophobia, which means--

DROPPO: Fear of clowns.

DOUG: Right.

DROPPO: So, I'm not sure this was a such a good idea for a birthday present.

DOUG: No, actually it's a great idea.

DROPPO: How do you figure?

DOUG: Well, how many pieces of jewelry can you get someone? And how many fancy restaurants can you go to? But this... to take someone's greatest fear and have them finally face it and overcome it, don't you think that's the best present you could ever give anyone? She can't go to the circus, can't go to carnivals, and she can't go to half the birthday parties for our nephews and nieces because there's going to be a clown there. It's an irrational fear that genuinely affects the quality of her life. So, what better present than curing her of that fear?

DROPPO: Right.

DOUG: Now, I did some research on

phobias and apparently what
the experts do to get people
over their fears is try to
get them more comfortable
with the very thing that
terrifies them. They call it
immersion therapy... which is
where you come in.

DROPPO: Yeah, I get that.

DOUG: So, what I'm going to do is,
I'm going to leave you two
alone for a little bit, and
run up to the store to get
some birthday candles. It'll
give Melissa time to...
assimilate, or whatever the
word is.

DROPPO: Acclimate?

DOUG: Bingo! Let her acclimate to
you being here and, you know,
once she gets over the shock,
just play it by ear. Okay?
Great! I'll be back in a few.

           <u>DOUG EXITS THROUGH
           FRONT DOOR.</u>

           <u>MELISSA CONTINUES TO
           WHIMPER.</u>

DROPPO: I'm really sorry about this.
Your husband didn't tell me
you were scared of clowns.
(SHE'S STILL WHIMPERING)
Listen—

           <u>DROPPO SQUEAKS FORWARD
           ANOTHER STEP CAUSING
           MELISSA TO WHIMPER EVEN
           LOUDER AND MOVE AWAY.</u>

Okay... maybe I'll just sit
down.

           <u>DROPPO SITS ON THE</u>

<u>SOFA. HE START LOOKING THROUGH ONE OF THE TRAVEL MAGAZINES.</u>

Lots of travel magazines here. The Greek Islands, huh? Do you like to travel? ... I've never been to Greece, or Europe even. I've been to Montreal though... that's kind of like Europe, so I've been told... (SIGHS, THEN GETS AN IDEA) Do you like magic tricks?

<u>SHUFFLES CARDS.</u>

<u>MELISSA SHAKES HER HEAD VIOLENTYLY, NEGATIVE GRUNTS.</u>

You know, I'm just a regular person in a costume, with some makeup on. I don't understand why people, and believe me, it's a lot of people these days, why they have such a problem with clowns. Just last week, I got hired for this birthday party, a kid's birthday party, and they told me explicitly that I couldn't come dressed as a clown. So, I go, you know, a gig's a gig, and I'm doing my thing, making balloon animals and whatnot, and I ask this one little girl why they wouldn't let me be a clown... that I'm a nice clown, a funny clown. And this girl says to me, "Because if you were a clown, I wouldn't be here right now." I mean, that hurts. It does. It's not like I just put on this outfit and call myself a clown. I went to Clown College... I did... studied the films of Charlie Chaplin and The Three Stooges. I can juggle, walk on stilts, I can ride a unicycle... I broke my left elbow twice learning how to walk in these clown shoes. And now, all of a sudden, I freak people out. Where did that come from? Somehow, we now live in a society where everyone's afraid of something all the time. Everyone has some kind of phobia, or allergy, or condition... if it's not on our phones or a TV screen, we're terrified. So, we do everything we can to avoid the real world and real people. Anyway, I'm sorry about this. I really am. But why people are so afraid of clowns... I just don't get it.

MELISSA: It was a parade...

DROPPO: Huh?

MELISSA: ...a Thanksgiving Day Parade. That's when it started.

DROPPO: Do you want to tell me about it?

MELISSA: I've never told anyone, ever... not even my husband.

DROPPO: Well, it's up to you. Feel free to tell me if you want. I'm not here to judge or anything... I'm just some clown.

MELISSA: I was probably eight or nine years old and I went down to the parade with my whole family... my mom and dad, my two little brothers, and we got there early so we had a perfect spot, right on the curb. And the parade starts and it's just wonderful. It's a gorgeous autumn day, they've got floats and balloons and marching bands, and then finally, at the very end, here comes Santa Claus. He's on this amazing red and green, tinsel-covered float and he's getting closer and closer, and one of his elves comes by and gives me a candy cane, and I'm holding the candy cane as Santa passes right in front of us and, I can't believe it, but Santa turns and looks at me. Not at my mom or dad, not at my brothers, he's looking right at me, and he puts his finger to the side of his nose and winks. At me. And I know that he knows what a good girl I've been and that this is going to be the best Christmas ever and it's like I'm floating on this cloud of pure joy and I turned to my brother to tell him what just happened and when I do there's this clown... this huge clown face about six inches from mine, and the clown says, "Merry Christmas, little lady!" (LONG BEAT) And I wet myself. Right there in the street. And I couldn't stop. My brothers are laughing, other people are pointing, and my parents are looking at me like they don't even know who I am. It was the single most horrible, humiliating moment of my entire life.

DROPPO: Wow... I don't know what to say.

MELISSA: And that's not the worst part. The worst part, and I didn't realize this until years later, the worst part is that when I turned and saw that clown... I had the most powerful orgasm of my entire life.

DROPPO: Okay... I didn't see that one coming.

MELISSA: That's what it was. That's why I couldn't control myself. I just went numb... head to foot. And ever since then, I've had this problem with clowns... and to be honest, I've had some other issues as well because of that moment. Not that my husband hasn't been great. He has. He's very, very understanding, and our relationship is just about perfect in every other way, but... it's like I have this mental block when it comes to...

DROPPO: I get it. You don't have to say another word.

MELISSA: Sorry to unload on you like this.

DROPPO: No, that's what I'm here for. Well, at least you're talking to me...that's something.

MELISSA: I guess so.

DROPPO: And you're looking at me without screaming. I'll take that as a positive. You're actually doing pretty good.

MELISSA: Thank you.

DROPPO: Then how about we try something? Maybe your husband's right. Maybe just getting a little more comfortable, more acclimated, would be a good idea. So, how about if I get up, and I'll just stand in the center of the room.

<u>DROPPO SQUEAKS TO THE CENTER OF THE ROOM.</u>

I won't make any sudden movements, and if you want to get any closer to me, then you can. And if not, that's perfectly fine.

MELISSA: Okay.

<u>SHE WALKS OVER TO HIM.</u>

<u>BREATHING HEAVY ALONG THE WAY.</u>

DROPPO: How we doing?

MELISSA: My heart's kind of pounding.

DROPPO: You want me to sit down again?

MELISSA: No. No, I need to be able to deal with this. Like you said, you're just a regular person in a costume. (BEAT)

Where do you buy clown shoes, anyway?

DROPPO: There's a company called Spears... Spears Speciality Shoes. They've been around forty years or so. Good outfit. Quality products. But not cheap, believe me... this is their tri-color full-length, lollipop model. These set me back $425 a pair.

MELISSA: And are there specialty clothes stores for clowns too?

DROPPO: Oh, you can find plenty of stuff on-line, but it's all pretty cheap. I prefer to make my own costumes.

<u>A JINGLE OF A BELL HAS MELISSA TOUCHES HIS PANT LEG.</u>

MELISSA: This is beautiful stitching.

DROPPO: Thank you. I take a lot of pride in it. Tailoring is kind of a dying art, you know... kind of like clowning, I guess.

MELISSA: I love this color.

DROPPO: Do you? It's my favorite too. I mean, it has to be bright, that's part of the whole clown thing, but I still think the right colors are what really pull an outfit together.

MELISSA: Absolutely. (BEAT) Did you make the horn too?

DROPPO: No, it's just a regular horn... old-fashioned bike

	horn. Probably made in China.
MELISSA:	Can I...?

> <u>MELISSA HONKS THE HORN.</u>
>
> <u>THEY BOTH LAUGH.</u>
> <u>EXCITEDLY.</u>

| DROPPO: | Whoa Nelly! Wasn't expecting that! |

> <u>MELISSA HONKS THE HORN</u>
> <u>REPEATEDLY AS THEY</u>
> <u>LAUGH HARDER AND</u>
> <u>HARDER.</u>
>
> <u>SHE STOPS HONKING AND</u>
> <u>THEY BOTH TRY AND GET</u>
> <u>THEIR BREATH BACK, BUT</u>
> <u>THE TEMPERATURE BETWEEN</u>
> <u>THEM KEEPS RISING.</u>

MELISSA:	This is the closest I've been to a clown since... and I don't feel frightened at all.
DROPPO:	Good... that's good... really, really good...
MELISSA:	What's your name?
DROPPO:	Droppo. Droppo the Clown. It's kind of my schtick, you know, that I'm clumsy... I drop things... Droppo...
MELISSA:	That's why you dropped your horn.
DROPPO:	That's why I dropped my... dropped my horn.
MELISSA:	Droppo?
DROPPO:	Yes?
MELISSA:	There's something I need to tell you...
DROPPO:	Oh?

MELISSA: I... love my husband very, very much... and he's probably on his way back from the store right now.

DROPPO: Sure. That makes sense. When people go to the store... they usually come back... from the store...

MELISSA: Yes, they do.

DROPPO: Then maybe I should go.

MELISSA: I think so... but thank you. For... everything.

DROPPO: No problem.

DROPPO SQUEAKS TOWARD THE FRONT DOOR.

MELISSA: Droppo?

DROPPO STOPS AND TURN.

Can I ask you one favor?

DROPPO: Name it.

MELISSA: This is going to sound ridiculous, but can I have your... nose. Your... BIG... red clown nose.

DROPPO: My big... oh yeah, yeah. Of course. Here ya go. In fact, take the horn too. You never know when you might need a clown horn. They're both yours. And I'm gonna say goodbye now Melissa.

MELISSA: Goodbye, Droppo.

DROPPO SQUEAKS OUT THE FRONT DOOR.

MELISSA SITS ON THE SOFA AND TURNS ON THE RADIO.

MUSIC CUE:
"LITTLE DUKE"

SHE HONKS THE HORN.
AMUSED.

DOUG: Hey, I just saw Droppo
            heading out. Tell me. How did
            it go?

MELISSA: Good. Really good. (BEAT) Can
            you sit down, hon?

DOUG: Why?

MELISSA: Because I have a present for
            you. For... both of us.

DOUG: Great! What is it? (SHE SHOWS
            HIM THE CLOWN NOSE) That's a
            clown nose. A big, red clown
            nose.

MELISSA: Yes it is.

CLOWN HORN HONKS.

DOUG: And a clown horn too! Look at
            that.

MELISSA: And a clown horn too. (BEAT)
            Will you put it on?

DOUG: Put it on? Oh, you mean the
            big red nose.

MELISSA: Yeah.

DOUG: Uh, sure. Maybe I'll just put
            it on for a second. That
            might be fun.

MELISSA: It might be.

DOUG: Should I put it on right now?

MELISSA: You should put it on right
            now.

DOUG: Allllright. (HE PUTS IT ON)
            There we go. How do I look?

<u>MELISSA STARTS KISSING HIM.</u>

Melissa, are you okay?

<u>HE STARTS KISSING BACK.</u>

<u>CLOWN HORN HONKS.</u>

<u>END OF PLAY</u>

Episode 4.16
COMMUNAL TABLE
(Release date: January 29, 2024)

Written by Jenny Lyn Bader.

Originally premiered as a stage play at the Ritz Theatre[13] (Haddon Township, NJ) in July 2023. The cast was Liz Mattera (Minna), Sara Viniar (Allie), and Brian K. Herrick (Gary). It was directed by Brian K. Herrick. An earlier version of the play was originally written for the invitational June Plays at Urban Stages[14] in New York City where it received a staged reading directed by Joan Kane and featuring Sarah Sirota (Minna), Laura Woyasz (Allie), and Jon Krupp (Gary).

Synopsis: Have you ever had to share a table in a café with the wrong people? On one summer afternoon in June, the day of the summer solstice, three characters end up at the same café table. Minna enjoys eavesdropping, but this time is different — this guy is getting so many things wrong, she may just need to interrupt. Gary loves meeting new people, but it looks like his latest flirtation is getting sabotaged. Allie has come here for some peace but she's unlikely to find any here.

<u>Audio Play Production</u>
Produced and directed by Jonathan Cook.
Cast: Elizabeth D. Moore (Allie); Shelby Lauren Smith (Minna);

Mickey Lay (Gary); and Jenny Lyn Bader (Voice of Siri).
Music Cues: "Nice and Easy" by Louis Adrien; and "Is Leroy On It", "Mordecai Promenade", "Frolic on the Avenue", "Nomad Shuffle", "The Roar", and "Whole Tony" by Southside Aces.

Author (Jenny Lyn Bader) commentary: I first wrote "Communal Table" as a short play for an invitational themed event at Urban Stages, "The June Plays." All the pieces had to be somehow connected to the month of June. I love assignments and find their constraints to be liberating. I guess having the whole month of June to play with didn't seem like enough of a constraint so I decided to narrow it down further and set it on the day of the summer solstice. Which got me thinking about how different planets and people behave in each other's orbits. And how we have to deal with sharing a universe. Or a communal table, a shared universe I keep exploring. Depending on how much time you want to spend at this table, I might even have a longer version of this play available for those who need one.

For licensing rights to the stage play version, please contact the playwright directly at jennylyn@post.harvard.edu / agent jtantleff@paradigmagency.com.

SCRIPT: COMMUNAL TABLE

CHARACTERS

ALLIE...   Chocolate enthusiast and day
                  trader.

MINNA...   Cosmos enthusiast. Works at a
                  Planetarium.

GARY...   A man getting a drink at a
                  café. Probably owns a dog.

SETTING

A café.

CAFÉ AMBIENCE.

MINNA: When you ordered your drink, did they ask you any questions about it?

ALLIE: No.

MINNA: Good.

ALLIE: Are you okay?

MINNA: Oh yeah, fine.

When this place first opened... they used to know my drink. Remember the days when you'd come into a café and they'd know your drink? Not that long ago.

ALLIE: Um, I—

MINNA: You're probably a little young. But I remember. They'd know my drink, what size, which sweeteners. They'd know

	that I want ice even in the winter. It's odd but I drink iced drinks all year round.
ALLIE:	(DELIGHTED) Oh you're kidding, I —
MINNA:	There's so much staff turnover now, no one knows my drink here anymore. It's not like I expect anything like that. But today when I order my medium iced latte, the barista asks me, and she's not the first one to ask... she says, "Do you want skim?"
ALLIE:	Huh.
MINNA:	As if "skim" is something to want. As if less is more. Skim used to be a special request. Like cinnamon sugar. Or extra foam. It was an extra! But now it's the norm. The staff here thinks all of us want it... as if we're all on one gigantic diet... And what I want to know is: when did skim become the default?
ALLIE:	(TRYING TO FOLLOW) The default? You mean like the default setting on a computer? The fallback setting... before you program it?
MINNA:	(PLEASED) Yeah, that's exactly what I mean! It's like you can't leave the house without someone asking if you want skim. UGH! (BEAT) It's just gonna be one of those days, isn't it?
ALLIE:	I hope not. I just really

	want a peaceful day.
MINNA:	You're nice.
ALLIE:	Thanks.
MINNA:	Now you're thanking me for your being nice. That's ridiculous. I bet you were well brought up. And all you want is a peaceful day, but you sat at the communal table. You really have faith in your fellow humans.
ALLIE:	There weren't any other seats available.
MINNA:	I try to be like you. And I can be, for a while. I can be so frickin' polite. But then, as things build up, over time... I reach a limit. Do you ever reach a limit? You don't, do you? You just keep it together.
ALLIE:	I try.

<u>MUSIC CUE:</u>
<u>"IS LEROY ON IT"</u>

| MINNA: | I try too! But then several thousand baristas ask me if I want skim and then one afternoon... poof. You know what? Now that we've had this conversation, I'm gonna be better. Not let stuff get to me. Someone like you is a good role model for someone like me. Thank you. |
| ALLIE: | You're welcome. |

<u>A MOMENT OF SILENCE.</u>

<u>ALLIE THEN STARTS TO</u>
<u>SIP HER DRINK AS MINNA</u>

<table>
<tr><td></td><td>INTERRUPTS AGAIN MAKING
ALLIE JOLT.</td></tr>
<tr><td>MINNA:</td><td>And why do I care so much? Why do I feel so offended? On behalf of a few percent fat. (REGISTERING ALLIE'S JOLT) Did I scare you? I didn't mean to... Sorry about that.</td></tr>
<tr><td>ALLIE:</td><td>It's okay.</td></tr>
<tr><td>MINNA:</td><td>I'm just thinking about this skim thing and I'm wondering if it's because people don't understand whole milk... they think "whole" means it's 100% fat. But do you know what percent fat is actually in whole milk?</td></tr>
<tr><td>ALLIE:</td><td>Yes.</td></tr>
<tr><td>MINNA:</td><td>(SURPRISED) You do?</td></tr>
<tr><td>ALLIE:</td><td>It's 3.25%.</td></tr>
<tr><td>MINNA:</td><td>Wow, are you a nutritionist or something?</td></tr>
<tr><td>ALLIE:</td><td>No, I just... have a good head for numbers.</td></tr>
<tr><td>MINNA:</td><td>Really! I was gonna say I heard it was between three and four... but... 3.25... you are good!</td></tr>
<tr><td>ALLIE:</td><td>Yeah that's the figure for the mean percentage by weight. I don't even know where I read that. Numbers stick with me. When I read them a couple of times... (CONFESSING) Or once. Unfortunately when I read a number, I don't forget it.</td></tr>
<tr><td>MINNA:</td><td>Why would that be that</td></tr>
</table>

	unfortunate?
ALLIE:	A lot of numbers are depressing. So they... make me sad.
MINNA:	I guess even the great stuff has a downside. But wow. If numbers stuck with me like that, I'd be, I don't know... making lots of money on the stock market or something.

<u>MINNA LAUGHS, ALLIE LAUGHS, AND THEN THERE'S SILENCE.</u>

I remember a number here and there. If it's important. But most numbers don't do that. Stick with me. Other things stick. I'm not an idiot. Ideas stick with me. Actually some of them refuse to go away. (BEAT) I don't only mean ideas about milkfat, though little things like that can sometimes set me off. It's usually more... ideas about the cosmos. The ideas that can really recalibrate your reality.

| ALLIE: | Right. I'm sure. |
| MINNA: | But don't even get me started on "I Can't Believe It's Not Butter." You know why? Because I can definitely believe it's not butter! |

<u>ALLIE CHUCKLES. AMUSED.</u>

That stuff is disgusting. Have you ever tried it? There is no way that it's butter. So why would someone not believe it?

ALLIE PASSIVELY AGREES.

	I can't tell whether you agree with me or whether you're just really the politest person I've ever met.
ALLIE:	Or both!
MINNA:	Or both! Touché. Nice meeting you. Have a good one.

THE CAFÉ DOOR OPENS AS GARY ENTERS.

ALLIE:	You too.

ALLIE GOES BACK TO TYPING.

MINNA GOES BACK TO READING HER NEWSPAPER.

GARY WALKS OVER TO THEIR TABLE.

GARY:	Beautiful day.
ALLIE:	Finally!
GARY:	That looks so good, is that whipped cream?
ALLIE:	Yeah this is the frozen hot chocolate with the whipped cream.
GARY:	Just what I was wondering. Thank you.

GARY WALKS AWAY.

ALLIE SIPS HER DRINK.

MUSIC CUE:
"MOREDCAI PROMENADE"

MINNA:	Do you know him?
ALLIE:	Never seen him before in my life.

MINNA: You think he really can't identify whipped cream?

ALLIE: He just wanted to know what I was having.

MINNA: Mmm.

ALLIE: Whaddya mean, Mmm?

MINNA: Just Mmm. Nothing.

           GARY RETURNS TO THEIR TABLE.

GARY: Yours looked so good. I got one too. Do you mind if I sit here?

ALLIE: Go ahead. It's a... communal table.

           GARY SLIDES OUT A CHAIR AND SITS.

           HE THEN ADDRESSES HIS WATCH.

GARY: Siri. Will you text Ivar that we are confirmed for four o'clock tomorrow.

SIRI: I have multiple results for Ivar.

GARY: The cell number. Thanks. (TO ALLIE) Sorry about that! If you don't do something when you remember, you forget.

ALLIE: I know how it is.

GARY: Is this your newspaper?

ALLIE: It's hers.

GARY: (TO MINNA) Mind if I look at the front section?

MINNA: Go ahead.

GARY: Thanks!

Can you believe 7-year-olds
are being recruited as
soldiers in Yemen?

ALLIE: I know. It's so awful. The
United Nations estimated that
10,000 people were killed
there in the last two years.
but they were off by a factor
of six. It's actually 60,223.

GARY: (CONFUSED) Are those figures
in this article?

ALLIE: No. I read it last week. And
then... There's so much
that's happening right now
that I can't believe. That's
why I need so much chocolate.

GARY: Oh yeah? How much?

ALLIE: I'm here at least twice a
day.

MINNA: (UNDER HER BREATH) I can't
believe she just told him
that.

GARY: So this is where you hang
out?

ALLIE: It's where I caffeinate.

Excuse me that's a client
email I have to deal with
right now.

MINNA: (UNDER HER BREATH) Good. Just
ignore him.

ALLIE:	Sorry about that.
MINNA:	(UNDER HER BREATH) Now she's apologizing?
GARY:	If you need to work, just ignore me.
ALLIE:	No, there was just something a little urgent. But fine now.
GARY:	What do you do?
ALLIE:	I'm a day trader.
GARY:	You must be very quick.
ALLIE:	Oh, if you are a day trader, you don't want to be someone who misses anything.
GARY:	Wow, that was very serious the way you said that. I got chills. You must scare the hell out of the people you trade with. So how does it work? You just buy and sell during the day, but you don't hold things overnight? Have I got that right?
ALLIE:	That's it.
GARY:	And you wouldn't you want to? Sometimes? Hold something overnight?
MINNA:	(UNDER HER BREATH) Oh my god. Really?
ALLIE:	You're talking about a more traditional kind of investing, where you assess the fundamental underlying value of the equities... I don't make those kinds of judgments. I look for little discrepancies in valuation that crop up minute by

	minute.
GARY:	Wow. Your time must be so important to you.
MINNA:	(UNDER HER BREATH) Sure it is, buddy.
ALLIE:	Of course. I savor every moment. Don't you?
GARY:	Yeah. But the market's closed, this must be your calm time of day, right?
ALLIE:	Well, it's closed here, but Singapore opens in a few hours, so I just had to get back to them about that but yes there's a little lull in between so... chocolate.
GARY:	You know chocolate's very good for you?
ALLIE:	It better be. I need a lot of it to function.
GARY:	Remember the famous story about how red wine was good for you on 60 Minutes?
ALLIE:	Oh sure, we studied that segment at business school! You know 22 million households watched it? And red wine sales went up 44%?
GARY:	I think chocolate is gonna be next.

<u>MUSIC CUE:</u>
<u>"FROLIC ON THE AVENUE"</u>

First they learn it's an anti-oxidant, and then that it enhances mood... I feel like next there's gonna be an official study on a news show. It's inevitable. So

here's my idea for you.
Giving it to you for free,
because I like you. You
should invest in chocolate
companies!

ALLIE: Thanks, but I don't do that
kind of long-term value
investing, I'm a day trader.

GARY: So you don't care about
value?

ALLIE: Of course I do. It's the most
important thing there is.
Worth... is... it's
worthless. Value is much
deeper. Much more important.
It's what you want to look
for in a stable company, a
stable government, a stable
human being.

GARY: But why wouldn't you invest
in it?

ALLIE: Because it's difficult to
assess right away. It's not
as predictable, unless you're
talking in the very long
term. If you're looking for a
way to increase your earnings
every day? I find financial
instruments are more
reliable. In the very short
term.

HER PHONE BUZZES.

Excuse me.

GARY: Singapore calling?

ALLIE: Shh. One sec.

MINNA: (UNDER HER BREATH) Dude, take
a hint.

ALLIE STARTS EXCITEDLY

<u>WRITING DOWN SOMETHING.</u>

GARY: Now you might think that because I have these great ideas about the market, that I'm an investor too, but...

ALLIE: Oh I can tell you're not. Real investors don't come up to me in cafés with ideas about places I should invest.

GARY: Right.

<u>HE SIPS HIS DRINK.</u>

<u>ALLIE BEGINS TYPING ON HER LAPTOP AGAIN.</u>

You think they filter the water here?

ALLIE: You know, I've wondered that! Hope so.

<u>TYPING AGAIN.</u>

GARY: It wouldn't be very hard for them, to put the water through one of those pitchers that removes all the particles.

ALLIE: You can also do that under the sink. I have an attachment under my sink.

GARY: You're kidding. I used to have a filter attachment outside my faucet, but under the sink — I've never heard of that. That's fascinating!

MINNA: (UNDER HER BREATH) Oh give me a break.

GARY: Is that the latest thing?

ALLIE: I don't think so. My mom had one at least ten years ago.

MINNA: (UNDER HER BREATH) Ugh! I can't take this. Where is my crossword puzzle?

SHE FLIPS THROUGH THE NEWSPAPER.

GARY: You enjoying the summer so far?

ALLIE: Oh yeah.

GARY: June is my favorite month.

ALLIE: Why's that?

GARY: I don't know, I like everything about it. I get along well with my father, and there's Father's Day. I like weddings, and there are often weddings.

ALLIE: You forgot Flag Day.

GARY: Flag Day. That's cute! I never would forget it. I like to celebrate that one.

ALLIE: Really?

GARY: And what I also love is today. The summer solstice. The way the sun suddenly gets going. Which gives us that summer solstice. Which is why, of course, it's the longest month.

MINNA: (ERUPTING) Oh stop! It is not the longest month!

GARY: What?

MINNA: (TO ALLIE) You don't have to talk to him!

ALLIE: I know that.

MINNA: I'm sorry, I just can't... anymore! I said nothing when

	you pretended not to know what whipped cream was.
ALLIE:	That's not exactly...
MINNA:	I said nothing when you gratuitously sent a text that you could have typed by speaking to your watch. To show her, to show all of us, you have the very latest model of that watch.
GARY:	What? It's a small screen! I always talk to it.
MINNA:	I allowed you a section of my newspaper and I listened while you used horrors happening in the world to further your personal agenda.
GARY:	Hey, that's...
MINNA:	When you basically got her to give you her schedule, I said nothing.
GARY:	Not fair. I know she's here twice a day. I have no idea when.
MINNA:	But I can't remain silent any longer in the face of the worst pick-up lines I have ever heard...
GARY:	They're not pick-up lines! I'm just being friendly!
MINNA:	Because your latest ones are not only bad, they're entirely wrong. June is not the longest month. It's actually one of the shorter months. It contains the longest day.
GARY:	That's what I meant.

MINNA:	I'll tell you what you meant. The longest day of the year takes place in June. On June 21st in this part of the world. Today! It's known as the summer solstice. You know why they call it that? Not because the sun "gets going." Solstice. Is from the Latin. Sol Stitium. Which means the Sun. Stands Still. It stops moving. Which is the opposite of getting going!
GARY:	You're being a little bit literal.
MINNA:	Astronomy? Is literal.
GARY:	I just meant the sun was doing its thing.
MINNA:	You can't go around spreading misinformation like that. This is the day the North Pole points directly at the sun, 23 degrees north latitude, so the noon sun appears at its highest point of the year. Nearly directly overheard.
ALLIE:	I noticed that today! That the sun was really high!
MINNA:	Very good. That's how summer begins. That angle is what makes this the longest day of the year.

MUSIC CUE:
"NOMAD SHUFFLE"

GARY:	(BITTERLY) Oh yeah? It's funny, I can think of another reason today feels like the longest day of the year.

MINNA: It's important not to confuse things. Did you know that on Venus, a day is longer than a year?

GARY: No.

MINNA: So many people get that wrong.

ALLIE: How can a day be longer than a year?

MINNA: Because a day means one spin around the axis. While a year means one orbit around the sun.

CRUMPLES UP TWO NAPKINS TO DEMONSTRATE.

So Earth is doing this. While Venus is doing that.

GARY: What are you, some kind of astronomer?

MINNA: I work at the Planetarium.

GARY: I love the Planetarium!

MINNA: You know, I would never have guessed that.

GARY: But that doesn't give you the right to interrupt. That was so rude.

MINNA: You were rude to the universe!

GARY: I was having a private conversation.

MINNA: At a communal table. While misrepresenting the cosmos.

ALLIE: (TO GARY) She's right. You were really imprecise. I should go.

<u>SHE PUTS AWAY HER
LAPTOP AND ZIPS UP HER
BAG AND STANDS.</u>

MINNA: You're very sensible.

ALLIE: (TO MINNA) And he's right, you are rude. And have been since you sat at my table and put your newspaper sections all over it. Don't you see it's insulting that you thought you had to help me? Do you think I'm incapable of protecting myself? That no one's ever hit on me in a café before? Do you think because I'm kind and responsive that I'm about to be emotionally manipulated by some guy I just met? That because he's flirting we can't have a civil conversation? That because he mentions a tragic child soldier situation to me that I'm going to be thinking I must follow this man to the ends of the earth because he cares about child soldiers? Have you considered that you shouldn't make so many assumptions about a person you don't know? That we all should not make assumptions about people we don't know? Just because we happen to be sharing a table with them? I really don't know why they make people share tables. We're not wired for it. So if you'll excuse me, I'm going to find a non-communal place to sit at where I can check in on my markets and drink my

> frozen hot chocolate in peace!

> ALLIE GRABS ALL THE NEWSPAPER SECTIONS

MINNA: That's my newspaper.

> ALLIE THROWS THE NESPAPER BACK ON TO THE TABLE AND STORMS OFF.

GARY: Hey don't go!

> GARY FOLLOWS HER.

> THE CAFÉ DOOR OPENS AND CLOSES INTO GARY'S FACE.

> GARY GRUNTS IN PAIN.

> HE RETURNS TO THE TABLE WITH MINNA.

She slammed the door. On my nose.

> MINNA TRIES NOT TO LAUGH.

I hope you're happy.

MINNA: No! It's just funny.

GARY: Maybe a little funny. Not what I was expecting. You were so harsh, I thought — what's your name?

MINNA: Minna.

GARY: Minna. Nice name. I'm Gary. I thought, I should bring this woman Minna around with me. Then when I try to meet a woman Minna can yell at me at just the right moment! And then the woman will have to come to my defense and take me into her arms. Not you.

	The woman. I mean.
MINNA:	As if I'm not a woman.
GARY:	No of course you are. I'm just imagining a theoretical woman who's open to meeting people.
MINNA:	Right.
GARY:	And then you could be my "wingwoman"!
MINNA:	I couldn't do that. Because I'd have to listen to you say those same lines all the time.
GARY:	I would never repeat lines.
MINNA:	Really? Those were made up specifically for her?
GARY:	Of course! I mean if a line was really good. Like "Sol Stitium," wow. Thanks for that one. I'm going to keep that for a rainy day. Or rather, a really sunny day. I guess I can only use that one on June 21st. Maybe next year.

<u>MUSIC CUE:</u>
<u>"THE ROAR"</u>

MINNA:	Oh Jesus. I gave you a line? I'm gonna be sick.
GARY:	Why? I'm not that bad. She was very happy talking to me! I said what I thought she would like — and she did, until you came along.
MINNA:	So how do you customize these? I mean, what would you say to me, rather than her?

GARY: You? I would never try to pick you up, you're a very hostile person.

MINNA: Good.

SHE SIPS HER DRINK.

GARY: But I'd love you to tell me more about the universe.

MINNA: No. Oh. No. No. And no.

GARY: No, really! Of everything that's happened this afternoon, that was the most interesting part. When you explained the universe in a way I'd never understood it. It was fascinating.

MINNA: "Fascinating"? Where have I heard that before? Oh it must have been when you were talking about the under-sink water filter. Tell me, is the universe more fascinating than the under-sink water filter?

GARY: A lot more fascinating, though they're similar.

MINNA: The universe is similar to the under-sink water filter. In the sense that they're both... bullshit?

GARY: No. It's because the hidden element, the parts we can't see, are the parts we most need to understand. We're all wearing blinders aren't we? All not seeing that all we can see is the earth way of thinking. Stuck with the mindset of one particular planet. We live in a

	universe, but we know only one world of it. When you were doing that demonstration with the crumpled-up napkins, I thought: We take so much for granted. We think it's so obvious a day is shorter than a year. We think of that... the "default."
MINNA:	(AMAZED) You mean... like the default setting of a computer? Before it's been reprogrammed?
GARY:	Yes, yes! That's what I mean! But then there's this other planet where a year can last longer than a day. Completely challenging the way we think about time.
MINNA:	Yes.
GARY:	Now, don't get me wrong, I don't usually like to have a default setting changed.
MINNA:	Oh, me neither.
GARY:	Like how taxis used to be default quiet but now they can't be...
MINNA:	(TOGETHER)Because Taxi TV is too loud.
GARY:	(TOGETHER)Because Taxi TV is too loud.
MINNA:	Who decided the TV should be turned on when you go in?
GARY:	And remember the time before carbs were evil? Getting a basket of rolls in a restaurant was the default. But now, you have to ask for rolls. Sometimes for each

	roll, one at a time.
MINNA:	Yeah you can't even assume bread anymore.
GARY:	I miss not having to ask for water too. Don't get me wrong... a water shortage is a terrible thing, and people who don't like water shouldn't get it automatically. But those of us who drink it... what a pleasure it was receiving a simple glass of water when we walked in. As if the restaurant knew us and understood us.
MINNA:	Yes, but with default beverages... the one that really gets to me is skim.
GARY:	Oh my god yes when did skim become the default?
MINNA:	I know!
GARY:	Why, when you order a cappuccino do they ask if you want skim? Don't you think I would have mentioned that up front?
MINNA:	Right?
GARY:	So yeah, I like most of the defaults we have, I get disoriented when they keep changing. But then there are others I wish would change!
MINNA:	Oh me too! The organ donation box on the driver's license! If it were just automatically checked —
GARY:	(TOGETHER) If the checked box were the default!

MINNA: (TOGETHER) If the checked box were the default!

GARY: And you had to uncheck it if you didn't want to donate.

MINNA: Think how many lives would be saved.

GARY: Then thinking about time...

MINNA: Time is so important to think about.

GARY: Yes. And we've divided it up in such a specific way. We set the clocks back, we set them forward, we have favorite months...

MINNA: We come in here between four and five...

GARY: We decide to make our own hours or waste time or divide it up into little pieces like that day trader we were just talking to. She has a job where she has to decide whether to buy or sell every second. We spend our whole lives in relationship to time and we don't realize how planet-specific that is...

                         MUSIC CUE:
                         "WHOLE TONY"

MINNA: How could we? Most people don't even look at other planets! And what might be going on there!

GARY: Just thinking about a planet where a day is longer than a year makes you question all your assumptions. Makes you think about the height of the sun and the tilt of the earth

in relation to your day. In
relation to all of your days.
I want that context, that
bigger conversation. You are
talking about the grand
scheme. Sure I'm very fond of
all the little conversations
we have in passing. I love
water filtration and number-
crunching and chocolate.
There are so many good
conversations to be had. But
they all pale in comparison
to the deepest conversation.
About the grand scheme of the
universe. Because it's...
vast and humbling in its
scope. Puts everything in
perspective.

MINNA: Do you think the people on
other planets are amazed by
how time works on earth?

GARY: If there is intelligent life
out there, of course they're
having this conversation.
They'd have to be. Thinking
about how the angles of light
and air, the relationship of
planetary systems to one
another, impacts our own
reality... It's the key
conversation. It changes the
way we have all the other
conversations.

MINNA: I hate to say it but I agree
with you. It's why I had to
interrupt. Your
mischaracterization of the
solstice was...

GARY: A violation of that! Of
course it was.

MINNA: I shouldn't have interrupted.
            But I'm glad you see my
            point. Nice talking to you.

                    MINNA GOES BACK TO
                    READING HER NEWSPAPER.

GARY: So. Can you explain, again,
            how Venus works?

MINNA: You really want to know how
            Venus works.

GARY: I'm getting the basic gist,
            but I'd like to understand it
            better.

MINNA: You mean, explain again with
            a crumpled-up napkin?

GARY: Actually, I own a dog so I
            happen to have a rubber ball.

                    HE PULLS A RUBBER BALL
                    FROM HIS POCKET AND
                    BOUNCES IT.

MINNA: To play fetch with?

GARY: On most days. He likes fetch.
            And on most days after our
            evening walk, we play fetch
            with this ball. But today,
            the longest day of the year,
            when the sun comes to a
            complete standstill, at a
            23.5-degree angle... this can
            be a planet.

                    END OF PLAY

____

Episode 4.17
FOR A LIMITED TIME ONLY
(THE BREAD PLAY)
(Release date: March 5, 2024)

Written by Daniel Prillaman.

Originally premiered as a stage play through The Feral Theatre Company at the Minnesota Fringe Festival[15] in August 2021. The production was directed by Isabella Dunsieth and assistant directed by Ahnika Collette. Lighting design and videography by Kati Hoehl, sound design by Isabella Dunsieth, and set design by Braden Joseph. Original cast – Haily Sky (Val); Christopher Jenkins (Arlo); and Daniel Collette (The Server).

Synopsis: After getting the unlimited bread deal at an Italian restaurant, Arlo and Val are both stuffed and ready for the check. But their server doesn't bring them their check. He brings them more bread. He keeps ... bringing them more bread. He won't stop. He won't ever stop. The bread is unlimited. And there is no escape. A romantic horror comedy about the hard truth that nothing lasts forever, except maybe bread.

<u>Audio Play Production</u>
Produced and directed by Jonathan Cook.
Cast: Roshelle Simpson (Val); John D. Nelson (Arlo); Valentin Angel

Fernandez (Server); with Jacquelyn Floyd Priskorn and Jonathan Cook (Advertisement Voices).
Music Cues: "Scherzetto", "La Luna e la Fisarmonica", "Piazza San Marco", "Schivola", and "Fantastico" by Ziv Moran; "Waltzing in Paris" and "Escape to Sicily" by Louis Adrien; "Fun in the Sun" by BalloonPlanet; and "Café de Manhã" by Luc Allieres.

Author (Daniel Prillaman) commentary: This is a play about bread. It's also probably about love and serenity. Or making the most of the moments you find yourself in.

But it's definitely about bread. I try to write the plays that I didn't know you could do in theatre when growing up, which means when I see a surreal meme on the internet about endless bread, I go, "well, that's a play," and see how far I can stretch and subvert the idea without killing it. Finding a story in it is a bonus. My wife and creative partner, Alli, and I see a lot of ourselves in Arlo and Val (we're both Pisces, it's gross), and I think neither of us would close this preamble without the words of fellow playwright Morey Norkin, "If there's a moral to the story, I think it's if you want to eat out, do it at home."

For licensing rights to this play, contact the playwright directly at danielprillaman@gmail.com.

SCRIPT: FOR A LIMITED TIME ONLY

CHARACTERS

ARLO...	Any adult age. Any ethnicity. Male.
VAL...	Any adult age. Any ethnicity. Female.
THE SERVER...	Any age. Any ethnicity. Any gender.
AD VOICES...	Voices on the advertisement.

SETTING

The dining room of the Italian Garden Factory.

This deal is, in fact, available for a limited time only.

<u>SCENE 1</u>

<u>QUIET MUSIC PLAYS OVER THE DINING ROOM SPEAKERS.</u>

<u>MUSIC CUE: "SCHERZETTO"</u>

<u>PLATES AND SILVERWARE CLINK.</u>

VAL: Oh my god.

ARLO: I am stuffed.

VAL: Me too.

ARLO: I literally don't feel like I can get up.

VAL: Well, start making room. We're gonna have to eventually.

ARLO: You don't think they'll, like, just let us sit here indefinitely?

VAL: Nope. You can only do that at home.

ARLO: We can dream.

VAL: Can we?

ARLO: Oh, yes. I long for the day when we can just sleep right in the restaurant.

VAL: Pretty sure you have to own the place to do that. And even then, you sleep on a different floor. Like, above it.

ARLO: Can you not crush my dreams for just a minute?

VAL: Nope. Besides, you can dream better dreams than just being able to sleep wherever you want.

ARLO: Can I?

VAL: Shut up.

ARLO: Love you.

VAL: I love you, too.

> VAL POKES AROUND AT THE REMAINING PIECE OF BREAD IN THE BASKET ON THEIR TABLE.

Can you handle that last piece of bread? 'Cause I don't know if I can.

ARLO: Uhhhhhh. Maybe.

> ARLO GRABS THE LAST PIECE.

> HE CHEWS.

Ohhh. Maybe not.

VAL: Here. Maybe I'm wrong.

> VAL GRABS THE BREAD.

> SHE TRIES... AND THEN SETS IT BACK DOWN.

Or maybe I'm right.

ARLO: It's like it's mocking us.

VAL: No.

ARLO: It's sneering. (AFFECTING A RIDICULOUS VOICE AS THE BREAD) "Finish me." "Finish meeeeeee." "I'm unlimited! Get your money's wooooooorth."

VAL: What are you doing?

ARLO: I'm being the bread.

VAL: Why?

ARLO: ...

VAL: We're in public.

ARLO: We're the only ones here.

VAL: Oh. Hey, what time do they close?

ARLO: Uh, I don't know.

<u>SERVER ARRIVES AT THEIR TABLE.</u>

THE SERVER: Hello, again, folks! More bread?

<u>ARLO AND VAL GROAN.</u>

(LAUGHS) Bit stuffed?

ARLO: More than a bit.

VAL: You aren't about to close are you?

THE SERVER: Hmm? Oh, no. Not at all! Looks like you two lovebirds have the place to yourselves. Relax as long as you want.

ARLO: (TO VAL) You hear that?

VAL: Thanks, um. We can probably go ahead and take care of the check though.

THE SERVER: You sure? No dessert? Coffee?

VAL: Thanks, no, the check is good. Could not eat another bite.

THE SERVER: You want a doggie bag for the bread? Don't want to let it go to waste.

ARLO: They've got a point.

VAL: Sure. That's fine.

THE SERVER: All right!

SETS DOWN A NEW BASKET
OF BREAD ON THE TABLE.

Well, I'll just leave this
fresh basket here while I go
fetch that. Just in case you
find a little more room in
the meantime. Get your
money's worth.

THE SERVER WALKS AWAY.

ARLO: They get it. $5.99.

VAL: Hell of a deal.

ARLO: Hell of a deal.

VAL: We should not have eaten this
much.

ARLO: Probably not.

VAL: The "get your money's worth,"
that's how they get you.

ARLO: Hell of a deal.

VAL: Hell of a deal. But it's
gonna ruin the whole night.

MUSIC CUE:
"LA LUNA E LA
FISARMONICO"

ARLO: You're not having a good
time?

VAL: No, I am, but it's all
downhill from here. We're
both gonna feel bloated and
sluggish the rest of the
evening. We'll get home and
plop down in front of the

T.V. to watch the latest episode of something we'll only pay attention to halfway because the other half is on our phones. We're not gonna have any energy to do anything else because we just ate our weight in carbs. You're also gonna use that as an excuse around 11 o'clock to say you're too lazy to fuck me. I'll say, "well, you could just go down on me." You'll make a pun which I won't laugh at about how you're still too full from dinner, and we'll wind up masturbating next to each other looking at our preferred style of porn, lesbian BDSM for me, and foot shit for you.

ARLO: Are you saying I don't go down on you enough?

VAL: Yes. But I'm also saying I think that I think unlimited bread deals cause more trouble than they're worth. I am digesting that idea now and forming that opinion.

ARLO: I can go down on you more. I like it.

VAL: Do it right now.

ARLO: What?

VAL: There's nobody here. Get under the table.

ARLO: Um...

VAL: I'm kidding.

          <u>ARLO LAUGHS.</u>

	I mean, if you want to, I won't stop you.
ARLO:	Well...
VAL:	You're too full from dinner?
ARLO:	(LAUGHS) Look, if this is a serious conversation, I want to take it seriously.
VAL:	I'm kidding.
ARLO:	It's okay if you're not. You always say, "every joke has a little bit of truth."
VAL:	I do say that. It's true.
ARLO:	Do you feel like I don't go down on you enough?
VAL:	I said yes earlier. You haven't gone down on me since.
ARLO:	(LAUGHS) I mean, I can go down on you more.
VAL:	Good.
ARLO:	I can't tell if you're messing with me or not.
VAL:	When in doubt, eat me out.

<u>THE SERVER ARRIVES AT THEIR TABLE.</u>

| THE SERVER: | Oh, that's a personal conversation. |

<u>HANDS THEM A TO-GO BOX.</u>

	Here is a to-go box for you, folks.
ARLO:	Thanks.
THE SERVER:	I hope I'm not overstepping my place, but I have to agree. If one partner's not

	pulling their weight downtown--
ARLO:	Oh, okay.
VAL:	Uh, where's the check?
THE SERVER:	Hmm?
VAL:	The check?
THE SERVER:	You want the check?
VAL:	We asked for the check.
THE SERVER:	You asked for the check?
VAL:	We did.
THE SERVER:	(REMEMBERING) Oh my god. You did! I am so sorry. Forgive me. I'll go get that right now. Be back in a jiff!

<u>THE SERVER WALKS AWAY.</u>

<u>ARLO BEGINS PUTTING THE BREAD IN THE TO-GO BOX.</u>

ARLO:	If it's that big a problem, I want to work to fix it, you know?
VAL:	We definitely asked for the check.
ARLO:	What? Oh. Yeah.
VAL:	More than once.
ARLO:	Yes? Oh. Cut them some slack, honey. It's a stressful job, they just forgot. It happens.
VAL:	We're the only ones here.
ARLO:	Yeah, but it's the end of a long day. They've been on their feet. Bunch of other people also probably took advantage of the bread deal. It happens.

VAL: Yeah. Still annoying.

ARLO: Fair enough. (BEAT) So what
                        do you want to do tonight?
                        (OVERLAPPING) I mean, I can
                        go down on you.

VAL: (OVERLAPPING) I want you to
                        fucking go down on me.

ARLO: Totally. I'm in. 100%.

VAL: Then maybe more Bake Off?

ARLO: Accents.

                        <u>VAL GRABS THE
                        UNFINISHED PIECE OF
                        BREAD.</u>

VAL: (IMPERSONATING PAUL HOLLYWOOD
                        FROM 'THE GREAT BRITISH BACK
                        OFF') See, there's a good
                        bake on this. Golden brown.
                        Looks a bit half eaten,
                        though. Did you eat this
                        before you brought it up
                        here?

ARLO: (JONING IN) Uh, I did.

                        <u>MUSIC CUE:
                        "PIAZZA SAN MARCO"</u>

VAL: Why would you do that?

ARLO: It looked good. I'm sorry.

VAL: You should be.

                        <u>VAL EATS THE LAST PIECE
                        OF BREAD.</u>

                        <u>CHEWING SLOWLY.
                        ADJUDICATING IT.</u>

                        I don't like it. I love it.

ARLO: Oh, thank God.

VAL: You're star baker.

ARLO: Oh, thank God. I'm going to
               go call my mum.

                    THEY LAUGH.

VAL: Oh my god, why did I eat
               that? Why did you let me do
               that?

ARLO: It was for the bit.

VAL: Ohhhh. Why do you let me do
               things for comedy that I
               wouldn't do otherwise?

ARLO: I don't know, I feel like I
               do a lot of things for comedy
               that I wouldn't do otherwise.

VAL: What is taking so long?

ARLO: I'm having a good time.

VAL: I am too. I just don't like
               waiting.

ARLO: They said to relax.

VAL: Mmm. Is it just me or is this
               place more... creepy than
               romantic? With no one else
               here?

ARLO: It's lots of space for
               activities.

VAL: I'm just ready to go home.

                    THE SERVER ARRIVES AT
                    THEIR TABLE.

THE SERVER: Hey, folks. Little bit of bad
               news, I am so sorry.

VAL: What is--

THE SERVER: We are actually having a
               little bit of a problem with
               our computer right now.

ARLO: Oh, no.

THE SERVER: I am so sorry, but your check
               is going to take just a
               little bit longer. I am so
               sorry.

ARLO: Well, that's okay. It
               happens.

VAL: Why'd you bring more bread?

THE SERVER: Hmm?

VAL: You're holding more bread.
               Why?

THE SERVER: Oh!

               <u>SETS THE BREADBASKET ON
               THE TABLE.</u>

               For you. As an offer of
               apology.

VAL: Oh. That's--you really don't
               have to.

THE SERVER: It's already made. No
               trouble.

VAL: We really couldn't eat
               another bite.

THE SERVER: If you don't, it's going to
               go to waste.

ARLO: Well, we'll eat it later. If
               we don't now.

THE SERVER: Okay! Great! Well. I'll go
               check on that check for you.
               Again, I am so sorry.

VAL: Uh-huh.

               <u>THE SERVER WALKS AWAY.</u>

ARLO: Okay, that interaction was a
               little more strangely
               pointed.

VAL: Are they fucking with us?

ARLO: Nooooo.

VAL: I think they're fucking with us.

ARLO: If their computer's broken, they literally can't do anything, though.

VAL: Is their computer broken?

ARLO: Val.

VAL: I'm just asking. Is it? We don't know. There's no one else here. Maybe this is how they get their kicks.

ARLO: I highly doubt that's the actual case.

VAL: They could do the check by hand. Computer just makes things faster.

ARLO: Well, when they come back we can ask them that.

VAL: You have any cash on you?

<u>ARLO CHECKS HIS WALLET.</u>

ARLO: Yeah. I have enough. We can ask them when they come back.

VAL: Okay. Thank you.

ARLO: I'm having a good night.

VAL: I am too. I'm just--I'm ready to be out of here, you know?

ARLO: Yeah.

VAL: I'm ready to be home.

ARLO: Yeah. I understand.

VAL: Okay. Thank you. I love you.

ARLO: I love you too. (BEAT) Want do you want to do with the bread?

VAL: Is there room in the box?

> ARLO LOOKS IN THE BOX.

ARLO: Not really.

VAL: Then we'll just leave it.

ARLO: Yeah.

VAL: It's clearly not our fault if
                  it doesn't get eaten. We've
                  made it clear we're full.

ARLO: Yeah.

VAL: It's not on us.

ARLO: Yeah. I know.

> THE SERVER ARRIVES AT
> THEIR TABLE.

THE SERVER: I am so sorry, folks.
                  Computer's still on the
                  fritz, but I have more bread!

> SERVER SETS DOWN A NEW
> BREAD BASKET ON THE
> TABLE.

VAL: What the fuck? Why?

THE SERVER: Hmm?

VAL: Why do you keep bringing us
                  bread?

THE SERVER: You ordered the unlimited
                  bread deal, silly. $5.99.

VAL: Yes, but we're done eating.
                  We're clearly done eating.
                  We're not going to eat more.

THE SERVER: If you don't, it'll go to
                  waste.

VAL: We don't care!

ARLO: Val--

VAL: Bring us our check, please.

THE SERVER: I would if I could, I am so sorry.

VAL: Then write it by hand. We'll pay with cash.

THE SERVER: I can't do that either, I'm so sorry.

VAL: Why not?

THE SERVER: Because I can't bring you your check until you finish the bread.

    MUSIC CUE:
    "WALTZING IN PARIS"

ARLO: What?

THE SERVER: If you want your check, eat the bread. Looks like you two are still working, so, I'll give you some more time. Just holler if you need anything!

    THE SERVER WALKS AWAY.

ARLO: Uh...

VAL: Fuck this.

    CHAIR SLIDES AS SHE STANDS.

    SHE GRABS HER COAT.

ARLO: Woah, wait.

VAL: Arlo, I don't know what's going on, but I am not staying here another minute. Come on.

ARLO: Okay. Yeah, this is weird.

    CHAIR SLIDES AS ARLO STANDS.

    HE GRABS THE TO-GO BOX.

VAL: Fucking leave the bread! Just

	come on!
ARLO:	It's gonna go to waste.
VAL:	Arlo!
ARLO:	Right. Yep. Sorry.

HE SETS DOWN THE TO-GO
BOX.

THEY BOTH WALK TOWARDS
WHERE THEY THINK THE
DOOR IS.

ADLIBS AS THEY WALK.

VAL SUDDENTLY STOPS.

VAL:	What the--
ARLO:	What?
VAL:	Where's the door?
ARLO:	What?
VAL:	Where is the fucking door?
ARLO:	What the hell?
VAL:	We came in from there.
ARLO:	Yeah. We did.
VAL:	Where's the-- What the fuck is going on?
ARLO:	The door's gone.
VAL:	I can see that!

VAL PANICS AND BREATHES
HEAVILY AS SHE WALKS
AROUND LOOKING FOR A
DOOR OR OTHER WAY OUT.

What the fuck? What the hell
what the fuck what the shit
the fuck? What the fuck?
There are no fucking windows
in this place!! No windows,
no doors, where did every way

	out of here fucking go?
ARLO:	Can we get out through the kitchen?
VAL:	We're about to find out.

<u>THEY BOTH QUICKLY WALK TO THE KITCHEN DOOR.</u>

<u>EERIE SWELL EFFECT FOLLOWED BY AN DOOR IMPACT AS THE SERVER APPEARS.</u>

THE SERVER:	I am so sorry, folks. (VOICE BEGINS TO DISTORT; DEMONIC) Only employees are allowed into the kitchen.
VAL:	What the fuck is going on?
THE SERVER:	(NORMAL VOICE AGAIN) Ma'am? I'm sorry, but I have to ask, can you tone down your language? The other customers?
VAL:	LIKE FUCK!
ARLO:	There's nobody else here.
THE SERVER:	Is there? (A CHEEKY BEAT) I'm just kidding. No, there isn't. But what is it you say, Val? (DISTORTED VOICE) "Every joke has a bit of truth?"
VAL:	Let us out of here. Right now.
THE SERVER:	(NORMAL VOICE AGAIN) I'm afraid I can't do that. Not until you both eat your bread.
VAL:	We are not eating any more fucking bread!

THE SERVER: Ma'am, again, please tone down your language. I don't want to have to ask you again.

VAL: Or what?

> AN EERIE SWELL AND THEN...

> SERVER GRABS VAL'S THROAT.

> THE MUSIC DRASTICALLY SLOWS DOWN AS THE TENSION RISES.

ARLO: Oh my god. Hey, put her down.

> VAL STRUGGLES TO BREATHE.

THE SERVER: (DISTORTED VOICE) Or I'll cut out your tongue, Val.

ARLO: Please put her down?

THE SERVER: (DISTORTED VOICE) And that would make it much more difficult to eat the bread.

> SERVER LETS GO OF VAL AND HER BODY DROPS TO THE FLOOR.

> MUSIC, HIS VOICE, AND THE SCENE RETURN TO NORMAL.

ARLO: Please. We just want to go home.

THE SERVER: You better start eating then.

> SERVER WALKS AWAY.

> EERIE STINGER AS THE SCENE ENDS.

<u>SCENE 2</u>

<u>ADVERTISEMENT MUSIC
CUE: "FUN IN THE SUN"</u>

AD VOICE #1:	Have you heard about the new unlimited bread deal?
AD VOICE #2:	Sounds expensive.
AD VOICE #1:	It's only $5.99!
AD VOICE #1:	$5.99?
AD VOICE #2:	$5.99!
AD VOICE #1:	OH FUCK!
SERVER VOICE:	That's right. Unlimited bread.
DEEP AD VOICE:	(PAN ACROSS) Un. Limited.
SERVER VOICE:	Here at the Italian Garden Factory, we give you all you can eat. Think we'll stop giving you bread like all those other restaurants? Hell no! For just $5.99, get unlimited bread with your meal. It's a hell of deal.
DEEP AD VOICE:	(PAN ACROSS) Hell of a deal.
SERVER VOICE:	Hell... I mean, The Italian Garden Factory. When you're here, you're eating bread. So come on down and join us. We'd love to put a smile on your face.

<u>MUSIC STINGER AS
ADVERTISEMENT ENDS.</u>

<u>SCENE 3</u>

<u>MUSIC CUE:
"FANTASTICO"</u>

<u>VAL AND ARLO, STILL IN</u>

<u>THE RESTAURANT,
STRUGGLE TO EAT MORE
BREAD.</u>

VAL: Oh my god. I'm okay. I'm okay. I'm not gonna throw up.

<u>SERVER ARRIVES AT THEIR
TABLE.</u>

<u>HE SETS ANOTHER BREAD
BASKET ON THE TABLE.</u>

THE SERVER: And here is some more bread for you! You folks doing okay? You need any more Diet Coke?

<u>VAL GAGS.</u>

Oh. Be careful. You don't want to have to eat it again if it comes up. Tastes a lot worse the second time.

ARLO: Why are you doing this?

THE SERVER: You ordered the unlimited bread deal. What do you think the word "unlimited" means? It means limitless, dear. Infinite.

ARLO: Then how are we ever supposed to eat all of it?

THE SERVER: (CHUCKLES) I'll be back with some more in a little bit. Enjoy!

<u>SERVER WALKS AWAY.</u>

VAL: We can't keep doing this.

<u>ARLO GROANS.</u>

We'll burst.

ARLO: Should we try and call someone again?

VAL: Did you suddenly get a signal?

ARLO: ... No.

VAL: Then no.

ARLO: What do we do?

VAL: When he comes back... You distract them.

ARLO: How?

VAL: I don't know. It doesn't matter. Just get him facing back towards the kitchen.

ARLO: Why?

VAL: So I stab him from the back instead of the front.

ARLO: What?

VAL: It's a bread knife, but it should do enough to give us time to run.

ARLO: You're talking about killing them?

VAL: Wounding. At best, probably.

ARLO: Val.

VAL: What other choice do we have?

ARLO: But that's--...

VAL: What?

ARLO: That's... violence.

VAL: Are you really debating ethics in this situation? Of all situations!

ARLO: You know I don't believe in violence. I'm a pacifist!

VAL: Then you should be fine since I'm the one doing the

	stabbing!
ARLO:	Val!

THE SERVER ARRIVES AT
THEIR TABLE.

THE SERVER:	Everything okay out here?
ARLO:	(TOGETHER) Yep.
VAL:	(TOGETHER) Yep.
THE SERVER:	Okay! Should be back with some more bread in just a bit!

THE SERVER WALKS AWAY.

| VAL: | Look, if you have any other suggestion, I am all ears. But drastic and existentially surreal situations call for drastic measures. Do you want to get home or not, Arlo? |

MUSIC CUE:
"ESCAPE TO SICILY"

ARLO:	Okay.
VAL:	Okay?
ARLO:	Okay. What do I say?
VAL:	Whatever you have to (WHISPERING) Okay, here they come. Let's do this.

THE SERVER ARRIVES AT
THEIR TABLE AND PLACES
ANOTHER BREADBASKET.

THE SERVER:	And here is some more! I do hope you two lovebirds are enjoying your evening.
ARLO:	(WITH WAY TOO MUCH EXUBERANCE) We are! So much!
THE SERVER:	Well, that's just great to hear!

ARLO: That's great to hear that you
                 think that's great to hear!

THE SERVER: Are you okay?

ARLO: (REALIZING IT WAS TOO MUCH)
                 Yeah! I'm fine. Uh...
                 Actually, I wanted to ask you
                 a favor.

THE SERVER: Anything! I'm here to serve!
                 What can I do for you?

ARLO: I was just wondering... we've
                 had so much bread. You know?

THE SERVER: I do.

ARLO: And, it's--it's been great.

THE SERVER: Our bakers are the best.

ARLO: But I kind of want to mix it
                 up a bit. As a surprise for
                 my partner.

THE SERVER: Oh! How sweet.

                          VAL ACCIDENTALLY DROPS
                          THE KNIFE.

                 Everything okay, Val?

VAL: Yep.

                          SHE PICKS UP THE
                          SILVERWARE.

THE SERVER: Great. (TO ARLO) You were
                 saying?

ARLO: Um, yeah. Could I order a
                 dessert?

THE SERVER: Oh, that is so sweet.
                 Unfortunately, our kitchen is
                 closed right now.

ARLO: What?

THE SERVER: Our kitchen is closed.

ARLO: But-- But...

<u>VAL STABS THE SERVER.</u>

<u>EERIE MUSIC BUILDS.</u>

<u>SERVER GRUNTS IN PAIN.</u>

VAL: Come on! Arlo!

<u>THEY RUN TOWARDS THE KITCHEN.</u>

ARLO: If the kitchen is closed, where's the bread coming from?!

<u>DOOR OPENS AND CLOSES TO THE KITCHEN.</u>

VAL: No. No! No! No no no no no no no no no no! FUCK! NO!

It's just a brick wall. It's the size of a closet. What the fuck is going on?

I'm dreaming. I'm dreaming. This is just a bad dream. This is a bad fucking dream.

<u>MUSIC DRASTICALLY SLOWS DOWN AS THE SERVER APPEARS.</u>

THE SERVER: You're not dreaming. If you were dreaming, you would've eaten all this bread by now.

<u>ARLO THROWS UP.</u>

Oh, Arlo. I did warn you. I'll go get you something to scoop it up. And a mint.

<u>THE SERVER WALKS AWAY.</u>

<u>PANICKED MUTTERINGS FROM ARLO AND VAL.</u>

<u>EERIE STINGER TO END SCENE.</u>

SCENE 4

TICKING CLOCK
TRANSITION TO SHOW A
PASSAGE OF TIME.

MUSIC CUE:
"CAFÉ DE MANHA"

ARLO: Should we try and call
someone again?

VAL: There's no signal.

ARLO: Can't you still call 911?
Even though you don't have
service?

VAL: You have to at least have a
SIGNAL. No signal means
nothing. You dumb fuck.

ARLO: Hey.

SCENE 5

TICKING CLOCK
TRANSITION TO SHOW A
PASSAGE OF TIME.

MUSIC CUE:
"CAFÉ DE MANHA"

ARLO GROANS
UNCOMFORTABLY.

VAL: Are you okay?

ARLO: I have to poop.

VAL: Then poop.

ARLO: Where?

VAL: I don't know! Pick a corner.

MORE GROANING FROM
ARLO.

What?

ARLO: What if they make eat me it?

<u>SCENE 6</u>

<u>TICKING CLOCK
TRANSITION TO SHOW A
PASSAGE OF TIME.</u>

<u>MUSIC CUE:
"CAFÉ DE MANHA"</u>

VAL: How many days has it been?

ARLO: I lost count.

VAL: Do you think anyone's looking
                        for us?

ARLO: Definitely. People notice
                        when people just...
                        disappear.

VAL: Do they?

ARLO: Yeah.

VAL: They're not going to find us.

ARLO: Don't say that.

VAL: It's true. ... I'm sorry I
                        called you a dumb fuck the
                        other week. However long it
                        was. I'm... (SHE BREAKS DOWN)

ARLO: It's okay. Hey. It's gonna be
                        okay.

VAL: How?

ARLO: I don't know. But it is.

<u>SERVER ARRIVES AT THE
TABLE CARRYING MORE
BREAD.</u>

THE SERVER: Hey folks! Here's some more
                        bread.

<u>SCENE 7</u>

<u>TICKING CLOCK
TRANSITION TO SHOW A
PASSAGE OF TIME.</u>

<u>MUSIC CUE:
"SCIVOLA"</u>

<u>VAL STARTS TO LAUGH.</u>

<u>AND THEN CONTINUES TO
LAUGH.</u>

ARLO: What?

<u>VAL JUST KEEPS
LAUGHING.</u>

What? Val?

VAL: The cat's probably dead.

<u>VAL KEEPS LAUGHING.</u>

<u>SCENE 8</u>

<u>TICKING CLOCK
TRANSITION TO SHOW A
PASSAGE OF TIME.</u>

<u>MUSIC CUE:
"SCIVOLA"</u>

THE SERVER: Happy three months, you two! You're sure you don't want any more Diet Coke?

VAL: I want to you die the most painful death mankind could ever conceive.

THE SERVER: Okay, well, there's no need to be rude, Ma'am. I don't make enough to put up with your attitude.

VAL: YOU SON OF A BITCH! I'M GONNA FUCKING KILL YOU!

CHAIR SLIDES AS SHE
STANDS AND ATTEMPTS TO
STRANGLE THE SERVER.

SERVER HITS VAL. WHAM!

SHE DROPS TO THE
GROUND.

ARLO: Hey! You didn't have to--

THE SERVER: Arlo, did you want a refill?

ARLO: Is she okay?

THE SERVER: Or ignore the question. That's fine, too. "Fuck me," right?

SERVER WALKS AWAY.

ARLO: Is--? Val?

SCENE 9

TICKING CLOCK
TRANSITION TO SHOW A
PASSAGE OF TIME.

MUSIC CUE:
"SCIVOLA"

VAL: Okay. Who got fired first? Me or you?

ARLO: Ooh. Definitely me.

VAL: Yeah.

ARLO: Your job likes you more than my job likes me. Liked. Um, I--

VAL: We should start working out.

ARLO: What?

VAL: All these carbs. Try to slow the weight gain.

ARLO: Right. Do you think we could

order other food? As time
goes by? Will they do that?

THE SERVER: When the kitchen is open,
yes.

ARLO: (OVERLAPPING) AAHHHH!

THE SERVER: But it will added to your
bill.

ARLO: WHERE DO YOU COME FROM?

SCENE 10

TICKING CLOCK
TRANSITION TO SHOW A
PASSAGE OF TIME.

MUSIC CUE:
"SCIVOLA"

VAL IS EXCERCISING
WHILE ARLO IS SLEEPING.

ARLO MUMBLES AS HE'S
HAVING HIS NIGHTMARE
AND THEN HE SUDDENLY
WAKES UP. TERRIFIED.

VAL: Hey! Hey! It's okay. It's
okay. It was just a dream. It
was just a bad dream.

ARLO: I dreamt we were in this
restaurant and they wouldn't
stop bringing us bread and--
(REALIZES WHERE HE IS) Fuck.
Oh goddamn it.

VAL: Yeah.

ARLO: Okay! Still want me to go
down on you?

VAL: Right now?

ARLO: What else are we ever going to do?

VAL: I mean, fuck yeah.

THE TABLE SLIDES, SILVERWARE CLINKS, AND THE TABLE CLOTH WHOOSHES AS ARLOS CLIMBS UNDER THE TABLE.

(AROUSED) Oh. Ohhh. Oh my god...

SCENE 11

TICKING CLOCK TRANSITION TO SHOW A PASSAGE OF TIME.

MUSIC CUE: "SCIVOLA"

VAL IS OUT OF BREATH; PANTING.

VAL: Oh my god. Oh my god, I love you.

ARLO: (CRYING) I love you too.

VAL: Are you crying?

ARLO: You don't taste like bread!

VAL LAUGHS AND CRIES.

SCENE 12

TICKING CLOCK TRANSITION TO SHOW A PASSAGE OF TIME.

MUSIC CUE: "SCIVOLA"

SHUFFLING FEET AS ARLO AND VAL DANCE.

<u>THEY LAUGH AND ENJOY THE MOMENT.</u>

<u>ADLIBS AS THEY STUMBLE INTO THEIR SURROUNDINGS.</u>

VAL: I forget how long it's been since I've danced.

ARLO: Maybe the wedding?

VAL: Maybe the wedding. Yeah.

ARLO: (BEAT) I don't get it.

VAL: What?

ARLO: What is this? Are we dead? Is this purgatory? Hell?

VAL: It can't be. If this was hell, we wouldn't be together.

THE SERVER: Sure you would.

<u>SCENE 13</u>

<u>TICKING CLOCK TRANSITION TO SHOW A PASSAGE OF TIME.</u>

<u>MUSIC CUE: "SCIVOLA"</u>

VAL: Your beard is starting to get really big.

ARLO: You think?

VAL: Too big.

ARLO: Aw. I kind of like it.

VAL: I do too, but moderation, you know. We should figure out a way to shave.

ARLO: We?

VAL: Your face ain't the only
                beard getting big.

ARLO: What? Ohhhhhh.

                SCENE 14

                    TICKING CLOCK
                    TRANSITION TO SHOW A
                    PASSAGE OF TIME.

                    MUSIC CUE:
                    "SCIVOLA"

ARLO: They're not going to sing,
                are they?

VAL: God, I hope not. I hate it
                when he sings.

ARLO: (SEES SERVER APPROACHING) Is
                that a cake?!

VAL: (REALIZING) He lit a candle
                on a breadstick.

ARLO: Fuck me.

VAL: Son of a bitch.

                    SERVER IS CLAPPING AS
                    HE APPROACHES.
                    PREPARING TO SING A
                    BIRTHDAY SONG.

THE SERVER: (SINGING) Happy happy
                birthday, from all the bread
                to you! Happy happy birthday,
                may your wishes all come
                true! Hey! Happy happy
                birthday, from all the bread
                to you!

                SCENE 15

                    TICKING CLOCK
                    TRANSITION TO SHOW A

	<u>PASSAGE OF TIME.</u>
	<u>MUSIC CUE: "SCHERZETTO"</u>
	<u>VAL IS IN LABOR. SHE PAINFULLY GROANS.</u>
VAL:	FUUUUUUUUUUUUCK!
ARLO:	You're doing great, Val! You're doing amazing!
VAL:	I KNOW I AM! HOLD MY HAND TIGHTER!
ARLO:	Ow.
THE SERVER:	Okay! Let's get this bun out of the oven, one more big push for me, okay?
VAL:	FUCK YOOOOOOOOOU!
	<u>VAL PUSHES.</u>
	<u>A NEWBORN INFANT IS HEARD CRYING.</u>
THE SERVER:	Congratulations! It's a girl!!
ARLO:	Oh my god!
VAL:	Can I hold her?
THE SERVER:	Of course!

<u>SCENE 16</u>

	<u>TICKING CLOCK TRANSITION TO SHOW A PASSAGE OF TIME.</u>
	<u>MUSIC CUE: "SCHERZETTO"</u>
VAL:	Okay. I think she's asleep. (BEAT) What?

ARLO: I had a dream last night.

VAL: Bad?

ARLO: No? I mean, it wasn't a nightmare. I guess.

VAL: You wanna tell me about it?

ARLO: Yeah. We were here. Still. In this place. But we had gotten old. Like, really old. Ancient. Like, shouldn't still be alive kind of old. We couldn't move by ourselves. The server was feeding us the bread like babies. With airplane noises.

VAL: (NOT ENTIRELY COMFORTED) That's a comforting thought.

ARLO: But we were happy, though. Content. I could tell. We were at peace. I don't know how, but we were.

VAL: What about the baby?

ARLO: ... I didn't see her. (STARTS TO BREAK DOWN) This is all my fault.

VAL: What?

ARLO: It's my fault.

VAL: No.

ARLO: No, it is! You wanted to go to Olive Garden.

VAL: Arlo.

ARLO: I said no, all their food is frozen. Let's go to the Italian Garden Factory.

VAL: Arlo.

ARLO: It's my fault.

VAL: Arlo. This is not your fault. Whatever this is, there is no possible way you did it.

ARLO: I don't know what's going to happen next.

VAL: Neither do I. But we'll get through it together. Okay? Okay?

ARLO: I'm sorry.

VAL: Don't be sorry.

ARLO: But I am sorry.

VAL: Don't be! Don't say that. We're trapped in some parallel bread world. Fuck being sorry. Fuck feeling bad. Fuck blame. Fuck--fuck bread! I can't--you can't put words to-- If this is our life now, so goddamn be it!

MUSIC CUE:
"LA LUNA E LA
FISARMONICA"

If we're gonna grow old and ancient as fuck in this claustrophobic, tacky ass wallpapered excuse for a dining room, eating basket after basket of bread that isn't Texas Roadhouse, no matter how hard you wish it was, if our arteries fucking turn black and carbonate because of all the Diet Coke, if we never see our families again or hold our loved ones, if this is our life now... I'm not going to live it any less than the fucking fullest I can. We deserve that. Don't be sorry. Don't give them

	that.
	<u>SERVER ARRIVES TO THE TABLE.</u>
THE SERVER:	Hey, there, folks! Here's some more bread for you.
	<u>PLACES ANOTHER BREADBASKET ON THE TABLE.</u>
VAL:	Thank you.
THE SERVER:	How are we doing with everything?
ARLO:	Good.
THE SERVER:	Well, that's great to hear!
	<u>SERVER SLIDES UP A CHAIR TO SIT NEXT TO THEM AT THE TABLE.</u>
VAL:	What's with the chair?
THE SERVER:	To be perfectly honest, I've been on my feet for a while now. I just wanted to sit while we talked.
VAL:	Talked about what?
THE SERVER:	Something has come up.
ARLO:	What?
THE SERVER:	As you are both aware, you had a child. Congratulations, again. Mazel tov.
ARLO AND VAL:	Thanks.
THE SERVER:	And therein lies the root of our talk. If you recall, you both ordered two unlimited bread deals.
ARLO:	Yes.
THE SERVER:	Well. Now there are three of

you.

A MOMENT AS THEY TAKE
THIS IN.

VAL: Does that--? What are you saying?

THE SERVER: It's time for one of you to go. You can't have three people taking advantage of two unlimited bread deals. Do you know how much trouble I would get in if I let that happen?

ARLO: You mean... go, like...

ARLO MAKES A CUTTING
THROAT VERBAL NOISE.

THE SERVER: Good Lord! No. No one's going to slit your throat with a bread knife. Go.

VAL: You mean just... "go?"

THE SERVER: Yes.

ARLO: "Go?"

THE SERVER: Go. Leave. Depart the establishment? "Go" is the simplest phrase. I thought it would be clear.

VAL'S BREATHING GETS
HEAVY WITH EXCITEMENT
AS SHE LAUGHS A LITTLE.

VAL: Just "go?"

THE SERVER: Yes! One of you needs to leave. This restaurant. Now. Don't look at me with those faces on your faces. Nothing lasts forever, dears. This shouldn't be a shock to you. Well, except for bread, of course. But everything else!

203

I'll give you a couple of
minutes to decide.

CHAIR SLIDES AS SERVER
STANDS.

HE WALKS AWAY FROM THE
TABLE.

A MOMENT AS THEY
CONSIDER WHAT HE JUST
SAID AND THEN...

ARLO AND VAL: (TO EACH OTHER) You should go.

ARLO: You don't deserve to be here.

VAL: Neither do you. Look me in the eyes and tell me you would handle whatever the rest of this is better than I will.

ARLO: I take offense at that.

VAL: That's exactly why you should be the one to go.

ARLO: Oh, yeah? Well, I--don't know what to say in response to that. But I'm not leaving. So... I guess you better get used to the idea.

VAL: Arlo.

ARLO: Because I'm not leaving. And if you're not leaving, then--

VAL: We can't.

ARLO: What if she was taken care of?

VAL: She would never know us.

ARLO: But it would give her a life. Outside of whatever the rest of this is. Is it the most ethical option to--

VAL: Are you really debating ethics in this situation?

ARLO: When else are you supposed to? I mean, it's either that or we--

VAL: (BEAT) What? Arlo.

ARLO: We order a third.

VAL: What?

ARLO: We order a third bread deal. And we all stay together. Ethically, I know, I guess it's just as... murky, I don't know. What do you think?

VAL: Do you remember when we first moved in together?

ARLO: Of course.

VAL: I had gotten the job at the hardware store. And I was working all those hours while you were still at home every day looking for places to apply.

ARLO: A lot of good the English degree did me.

VAL: That was the first time we really spent a lot of time apart.

ARLO: Yeah. I missed you.

VAL: I missed you.

ARLO: I remember thinking every morning you walked out the door, "Oh my god, what if that was the last time we ever speak to each other? What if some... horrible accident happens? What if I

	lose her?"
VAL:	That's a little dramatic.

<u>MUSIC CUE:</u>
<u>"SCHIVOLA"</u>

ARLO:	I can't bear the thought of being without you.
VAL:	I love you, too. (EXHALES) Hell of a deal.
ARLO:	Hell of a deal.

<u>THE SERVER RETURNS TO</u>
<u>THE TABLE.</u>

THE SERVER:	All right! Have you two decided? Or do you need a few more minutes?
VAL:	No, I think we're ready.
THE SERVER:	Great! What'll it be?

<u>END OF PLAY</u>

Episode 4.18
UNKNOWN NUMBER
(Release date: March 27, 2024)

Written by Greg Mandryk.

Originally premiered as a stage play at Blank Canvas Theatre[16] in Cleveland, OH in September 2018. Directed by Kevin Joseph Kelly with the following cast: Samantha Cocco (Samantha); Tiffany Trapnell (Mom); Eli Ravenson (Dad); Eva Nel Brettrager (Dispatcher); and Antonio DeJesus (Joe).

Synopsis: As a snowstorm rages outside, a woman receives phone calls from an entity that attempts to lure her outside.

<u>Audio Play Production</u>
Produced by RubySky Productions.
Directed by Christopher Plumridge.
Cast: Jacquie Floyd (Samantha); Barbara Guinan (Mom); Morey Norkin (Dad); Scott C. Sickles (Dispatcher); Dana Hall (Operator); and Christopher Plumridge (Joe).
Music Cues: None.

Author (Greg Mandryk) commentary: We know vampires can't enter a home without being invited and sunlight will blast them out of existence. Silver is an anathema to werewolves who can only assume their bestial forms by moonlight. Dealing with zombies? Aim for the head and don't get bitten. Modern horror audiences are well-versed in monster lore. When a classic beast from myth and folklore makes an appearance, we're forearmed, even if the hapless characters aren't. We know the rules. With Unknown Number, I wanted a monster who plays by rules we're as unaware of as our menaced protagonist is. And I've always felt a chill up my spine at the sound of howling winter breeze.

For licensing rights to this play, contact the playwright directly at gregmandryk@yahoo.com.

SCRIPT: UNKONWN NUMBER

CHARACTERS

SAMANTHA...	Woman at home.
MOM...	Mother of Samantha.
DAD...	Father of Samantha.
DISPATCHER...	Police dispatcher.
OPERATOR...	Operator. Any gender.
JOE...	Samantha's ex-husband.

SETTING

Samantha's Livingroom.
A snowstorm rages outside.

SCENE 1

EERIE TONES INTRO.

A SNOWSTORM WITH HIGH WINDS CAN BE HEARD OUTSIDE.

SAMANTHA IS SPEAKING ON A PHONE AS SHE WALKS

<u>AROUND THE ROOM.</u>

SAMANTHA:	I don't know. It's only an hour layover. I might have time to grab a quick dinner at the airport. It depends on how far I have to run to change gates.
MOM:	(FROM PHONE) Won't they give you anything on the plane?
SAMANTHA:	It's a two-hour flight. I'll be lucky If they throw me a biscotti.
MOM:	(FROM PHONE) Well, when you get in, I'll take you out to dinner. My treat.
SAMANTHA:	Thanks, Mom.
MOM:	(FROM PHONE) It'll be nice having you home again.
SAMANTHA:	It'll be nice getting away from here, especially with the way this winter's been. It hit full force about three weeks ago and hasn't let up.
MOM:	(FROM PHONE) It's been a little chilly down here, too. It only got up to 70 yesterday. (CHORTLES)
SAMANTHA:	Har dee frickin' har, Mom. So, I'll call you when the plane touches down.
MOM:	(FROM PHONE) Okay.
SAMANTHA:	And thanks. I've needed this. The past month has been... Well, it's been something.
MOM:	(FROM PHONE) I know, sweetheart. I'm always here for you.

SAMANTHA: Thank you, Mom.

MOM: (FROM PHONE) Have a safe trip. I'll see you tomorrow.

SAMANTHA: I love you.

MOM: (FROM PHONE) I love you, too, dear. Good night.

SAMANTHA: Night.

> SAMANTHA HANGS UP THE PHONE AND WALKS AWAY.
>
> THE PHONE BEGINS TO RING AGAIN.
>
> SHE WALKS BACK TO IT AND ANSWERS.

SAMANTHA: Hello?

MOM: (FROM PHONE) Hello, dear.

SAMANTHA: Mom. Weird. My phone didn't recognize your number.

MOM: (FROM PHONE) It's me, dear.

SAMANTHA: Yes, I know. What's up? Did you forget something?

MOM: (FROM PHONE) I love you, sweetheart.

SAMANTHA: I love you, too, Mom. (SILENCE) Mom?

MOM: (FROM PHONE) I need help.

SAMANTHA: Okay, what... What do you need?

MOM: (FROM PHONE) Will you help me?

SAMANTHA: Mom, are you okay?

> SILENCE.

MOM: (FROM PHONE) Go outside, dear.

<table>
<tr><td></td><td>THE WIND PICKS UP OUTSIDE.</td></tr>
<tr><td>SAMANTHA:</td><td>What?</td></tr>
<tr><td>MOM:</td><td>(FROM PHONE) Please. Go outside, dear.</td></tr>
<tr><td>SAMANTHA:</td><td>Are you alright, Mom?</td></tr>
<tr><td></td><td>NO RESPONSE.

THEN THE PHONE DISCONNECTS.

AFTER A MOMENT, SHE DIALS HER MOM'S NUMBER AND WE HEAR THE OTHER END RINGING.</td></tr>
<tr><td>DAD:</td><td>(ANSWERING MACHINE) Hello. This is the Martin residence. No one is here to take your call. But leave your name and number and we'll get back to you as soon as possible.</td></tr>
<tr><td></td><td>BEEP.</td></tr>
<tr><td>SAMANTHA:</td><td>Hey, Mom. It's me. Listen, I know this is a weird question, but did you just call me a moment ago? I mean, after we talked about tomorrow? Also, is this the old tape recorder answering machine? You might wanna upgrade. It's a little weird calling and getting Dad's voice. So... yeah. Call me back. Alright? Love you.</td></tr>
<tr><td></td><td>SHE ENDS THE CALL.

AS SOON AS SHE HANGS UP, THE PHONE IMMEDIATELY BEGINS RINGING.

SHE ANSWERS.</td></tr>
</table>

SAMANTHA: Hello?

                         PAUSE.

DAD: (FROM PHONE) Hello,
                 sweetheart.

SAMANTHA: Who is this?

DAD: (FROM PHONE) It's me.

SAMANTHA: No, it's not. Who the hell
                 are you?

DAD: (FROM PHONE) I need you to go
                 outside.

SAMANTHA: I know don't know why, or
                 how, you're doing this, but-

                         SHE IS CUT OFF BY THE
                         THREE TONES OF THE
                         "NUMBER DISCONNECTED
                         MESSAGE".

OPERATOR: "The number you are trying to
                 reach, 9-9-"

                         THE RECORDING
                         CONTINUES, BUT THE
                         VOICE IS SCRAMBLED, IT
                         SOUNDS HARSH AND
                         INCOHERENT.

                         SAMANTHA DISCONNECTS
                         AND DIALS FOR THE
                         POLICE.

DISPATCHER: (FROM PHONE) Bronson Police
                 Department.

SAMANTHA: Hello. I was wondering if you
                 could maybe send a patrol car
                 over to 1648 Bell Drive.

                         SHE SLIGHTLY SLIDES
                         OPEN THE CURTAINS TO
                         TAKE A PEEK OUTSIDE.

                 I... I think there may be
                 someone lurking around

	outside my house.
DISPATCHER:	(FROM PHONE) Have you seen anyone?
SAMANTHA:	(FROM PHONE) No. But I've been getting these calls. Prank calls. They keep telling me to go outside.
DISPATCHER:	(FROM PHONE) Would you describe the calls as threatening?
SAMANTHA:	I feel threatened, yes.
DISPATCHER:	(FROM PHONE) Have they made any threats against you?
SAMANTHA:	Not exactly. But I don't think they're trying to be funny. Also, I don't know how they're doing it, but...
DISPATCHER:	(FROM PHONE) Ma'am?
SAMANTHA:	Look, if there is a patrol car in the area, I'd really appreciate it if they could drive by, maybe flash the lights a bit. You know, in case there's somebody out there, they'll know to knock it off.
DISPATCHER:	(FROM PHONE) I'll see if there is a black and white in the area.
SAMANTHA:	(FROM PHONE) Great. So, about how long?
DISPATCHER:	Ma'am, the storm has all emergency services stretched pretty thin at the moment. It could be several hours...
SAMANTHA:	(FROM PHONE) Hours?
DISPATCHER:	(FROM PHONE) In the meantime,

	you can call your provider to see about having the number blocked. And if you should see or hear anyone outside your home, call 9-1-1 immediately.
SAMANTHA:	Great. Thanks for the pro tip.
DISPATCHER:	(FROM PHONE) You have a good night, ma'am.
	<u>SAMANTHA HANGS UP.</u>
SAMANTHA:	Useless...
	<u>SHE CLOSES THE CURTAIN BACK.</u>
	<u>THE PHONE BEGINS RINGING AGAN.</u>
	Talk to voicemail, asshole.
	<u>SAMANTHA EXITS THE ROOM DOWN A HALLWAY.</u>
	<u>AFTER A FEW RINGS, THE PHONE GOES TO VOICEMAIL.</u>
SAMANTHA'S VOICE:	(ANSWERING MACHINE) Hi, you've reached Sam's voicemail. Leave a message.
	<u>BEEP.</u>
	<u>SILENCE.</u>
	<u>SAMANTHA REENTERS CARRYING A METAL LOCKBOX.</u>
	<u>SHE STARTS TO OPEN THE LOCKBOX WHEN SUDDENLY...</u>
MOM:	(FROM ANSWERING MACHINE) We're waiting.

<u>SAMANTHA GASPS.</u>

<u>SHE QUICKLY GRABS THE PHONE TO MAKE SURE ITS DISCONNECTED.</u>

<u>THE WINDS CONTINUE TO GROW OUTSIDE.</u>

<u>THE DOOR RATTLES.</u>

<u>AFTER A BEAT, SAMANTHA DIALS A NUMBER AND IT BEGINS TO RING ON THE OTHER SIDE.</u>

JOE: (FROM PHONE; NOT PLEASED) Hey.

SAMANTHA: Please don't hang up.

JOE: (FROM PHONE) You need something?

SAMANTHA: Joe, I... Know what? This was probably a mistake.

JOE: (FROM PHONE) Yes, I'd say the odds are highly in favor of this being a mistake.

SAMANTHA: I just really...

JOE: (FROM PHONE) What? (BEAT) Okay, I'm hanging up.

SAMANTHA: I think I'm in trouble.

JOE: (FROM PHONE; SIGHS) What kind of trouble?

SAMANTHA: Some crazy person keeps calling me.

JOE: (FROM PHONE) I know the feeling.

SAMANTHA: Great. I really need you to be a dick right now.

JOE: (FROM PHONE) Okay, okay. So... what? You have a prank

caller?

SAMANTHA: It might be more than that. I think they're outside my house.

<u>SHE PEEKS OUT THE WINDOW CURTAINS AGAIN.</u>

JOE: (FROM PHONE) Outside your house? Right now?

SAMANTHA: Yes.

JOE: (FROM PHONE; LAUGHS) Sam, do you know how cold it is right now? It's freeze-your-nuts-off below zero out.

SAMANTHA: I know, but still...

JOE: (FROM PHONE) Did you call the police?

SAMANTHA: Yes. Surprise. You weren't the first person I thought of for help. They might send a car by in a few hours. That's it. They also suggested having the number blocked, but it's a different number every time they call.

JOE: (FROM PHONE) And so, you want me to come over in the middle of the worst storm of the year to scare off the boogeyman?

SAMANTHA: I'm sorry, Joe. I'm a little freaked out here.

JOE: (FROM PHONE) Sam, never having to worry about your latest drama is the only thing I got from the divorce. Okay? You got the house. You got the cat. All I got was to be... disinherited from you and your problems. Please, don't take that away from me.

SAMANTHA: Some lunatic is out to get me, Joe.

JOE: (FROM PHONE) It's all in your head, Sam.

SAMANTHA: This is real!

JOE: (FROM PHONE) I didn't say it wasn't real. I just said it was in your head.

SAMANTHA: I'm not crazy, Joe.

JOE: (FROM PHONE) You're functional, Sam. That's not the same thing. Or, at least, you were functional. (BEAT) I heard about the job. I'm sorry. And I know you don't want to hear it, but get yourself some help. You're turning into a real train wreck.

SAMANTHA: Joe?

JOE: (FROM PHONE) Yeah?

SAMANTHA: Your cat died.

JOE: (FROM PHONE) Aw, seriousl-?!!

SAMANTHA HANGS UP.

SHE OPENS THE METAL LOCKBOX.

THE PHONE RINGS AGAIN.

SHE IGNORES IT.

SUDDENLY THERE'S A BANG ON THE DOOR.

SAMANTHA GASPS.

EERIE AMBIENT TONES RISE.

SAMANTHA: Hello?

BEAT.

MOM: (OUTSIDE THE DOOR) Hello,
               dear.

SAMANTHA: I'm not crazy.

THE FRONT DOOR BEGINS
TO SHAKE AND RATTLE
LIKE SOMEONE IS TRYING
TO GET IN... OR IS IT
THE WIND?

MOM: (OUTSIDE THE DOOR) We know,
               dear.

SAMANTHA: Who is this?

MOM: (OUTSIDE THE DOOR) It's me,
               dear. Come outside.

SAMANTHA: You're not her. Who are you?

DAD: (OUTSIDE THE DOOR)
               Sweetheart, it's me. We need
               you to listen.

SAMANTHA: He's dead. Who the hell are
               you?

DISPATCHER: (OUTSIDE THE DOOR) Ma'am, I'm
               going to need you to step
               outside.

JOE: (OUTSIDE THE DOOR) You are
               crazy, Sam. I'm sorry.

SAMANTHA: How are you doing this?

OPERATOR: (OUTSIDE THE DOOR) The number
               you are trying to reach, go-
               out-side, is unavailable.

DAD: (OUTSIDE THE DOOR) Open the
               door, sweetheart.

SAMANTHA: (ALMOST IN TEARS) Why are you
               doing this?

MOM: (OUTSIDE THE DOOR) I'm so

	cold out here.
DAD:	(OUTSIDE THE DOOR) Let your mom in, darling.
JOE:	(OUTSIDE THE DOOR) Your mom's freezing her nuts off out there.
DISPATCHER:	(OUTSIDE THE DOOR) Ma'am please just open the door.
MOM:	(OUTSIDE THE DOOR) We're waiting for you.
SAMANTHA:	Stop it!
DAD:	(OUTSIDE THE DOOR) We just need you to open the door.
JOE:	(OUTSIDE THE DOOR) Open it, Sam.
DISPATCHER:	(OUTSIDE THE DOOR) Ma'am, the black and white is waiting for you outside.
MOM:	(OUTSIDE THE DOOR) Please, dear...
JOE:	(OUTSIDE THE DOOR) Sam...
DAD:	(OUTSIDE THE DOOR) Sweetheart...
	ALL THE VOICES BEGIN SAYING "LET ME IN" REPEATEDLY.
	THE DOOR IS VILOENTLY SHAKING AND RATTLING.
	AN EERIE SWELL AND THEN ALL THE VOICES AND NOISES STOP.
SAMANTHA:	Fine!!
	SAMANTHA OPENS THE LOCKBOX AND PULLS OUT A GUN.

SHE COCKS IT.

Be right out.

SAMANTHA WALKS TO THE
DOOR, GUN IN HAND.

SHE OPENS THE DOOR.

THE WIND MIRACULOUSLY
DIES DOWN AND WE HEAR
SUNNY DAY OUTSIDE
AMBIENCE - BIRDS, ETC.

What?

SUDDENLY, THE WIND
PICKS UP AND THE
SNOWSTORM IS BACK.

SAMANTHA GASPS LIKE
SOMETHING IS COMING FOR
HER.

SHE TRIES TO RUN BACK
INSIDE BUT THE DOOR
SLAMS SHUT.

WE THEN HEAR HER
BANGING ON THE DOOR
TRYING TO GET IN.

EERIE RISER AS SHE
CONTINUES BANGING.

SCENE 2

BACK INSIDE.

THE SNOWSTORM
CONTINUES.

THE PHONE RINGS A FEW
TIMES AND THEN THE
ANSWERING MACHINE
CATCHES IT.

SAMANTHA'S VOICE: (ANSWERING MACHINE) Hi.
You've reached Sam's

voicemail. Leave a message.

<u>BEEP.</u>

MOM: (FROM PHONE) Sam? It's your mother. I just got your message. Is everything okay? You seemed worried.

<u>SAMANTHA PICKS UP THE PHONE.</u>

SAMANTHA: Hello?

<u>EERIE AMBIENT TONES BEGIN.</u>

MOM: (FROM PHONE) Sam? Are you okay?

SAMANTHA: I'm fine. (BEAT) I love you.

<u>END OF PLAY</u>

Episode 4.19
THAT NIGHT 'BUTCHER' PETE GOT KNOCKED OUT BY JESSIE 'THE CANON' TESORI
(Release date: April 15, 2024)

Written by Jonathan Cook.

Originally premiered as a stage play at Le Chat Noir in Augusta, GA as part of their 8th Annual Quickies Play Festival in April 2017. Directed by Jonathan Cook. Original cast – Tom Colechin (Butcher Pete); Analeesa Rogers (Jessie Tesori); and Robbie Cook (Mikey B.).

Synopsis: World class heavyweight champion fighter, "Butcher" Pete Wilcox, is at the peak of his career – a living legend with a winning streak to brag about. He never expected, however, that his undefeated record would end in an exhibition match with Jessie "The Cannon" Tesori – a lightweight contender from the women's fighting division.

Audio Play Production
Produced and directed by Jonathan Cook.
Cast: Ian Russell (Butcher Pete); Bonnie Marie Williams (Jessie Tesori); Robb Smith (Mikey B.); Jonathan Cook (Announcer 1); and Valentin Angel Fernandez (Announcer 2).
Music Cues: "Bionic Games" by Ian Post.

Author (Jonathan Cook) commentary: When I first got the idea for this play, I remember there being controversy in the news and social media about there being considerations for women and men to be allowed to participate in the same sports divisions. Many felt that there was an unfair advantage in the world of boxing if men and women fought each other. So my brain started working. I've seen some tough women in my lifetime, so I created this tough sassy lady named Jessie who was just like these other tough women I'd seen before and put her up against a man. But not just any man. I wanted to raise the stakes. This was the Heavyweight Champion. A tough British bruiser named "Butcher" Pete (and yes, that is a subtle nod to the song "Butcher Pete" written by Roy Brown).

In the match, Jessie knocks him out in the second round, which bruises this Brit's ego. And I liked the idea of Jessie knocking him out so easily that she couldn't even believe it herself and from there the story just spoke to me as I wrote. Butcher may have been defeated but he's smart and he seizes the opportunity to make her believe he took a fall because if she can't even believe she had an honest win, then it'll be easy to make the fans believe that as well.

When this play was first staged, the cast was very dynamic. Butcher was played by a hulking British actor and Jessie was played by Analeesa Rogers who is a very small framed lady. The visual of their contrasting sizes made the story more compelling as well as added a bit of humor. Not something we could recreate in the audio play version.

For licensing rights to this play, contact the playwright directly at jonathanrcook@gmail.com.

SCRIPT: THAT NIGHT 'BUTCHER' PETE GOT KNOCKED OUT BY JESSIE 'THE CANON' TESORI

CHARACTERS

'BUTCHER' PETE...   Male boxer in his 30's. British accent.

JESSIE 'THE CANON' TESORI... Female boxer in her 20's. Should have some attitude.

MIKEY B....   Male in his 50's or later.
                     Pete's trainer. He is stern,
                     but should never come off as
                     mean to Pete.

<u>SETTING</u>

The locker room of an arena in some place
called Mayor's Income, Tennessee.

<u>SCENE 1</u>

<u>ROARING AUDIENCE.</u>

<u>ARENA BELL RINGS.</u>

<u>BOXING GLOVES LANDING
HITS.</u>

ANNOUNCER 1:   The Champ is looking rough
                     going into round two, Jim.

ANNOUNCER 2:   That first round was brutal.
                     I've never seen anything like
                     it.

<u>BOXING GLOVES LAND
SEVERAL PUNCHES.</u>

ANNOUNCER 1:   And look at that! Jessie is
                     completely unstoppable right
                     now!

<u>MORE HITS.</u>

                     Oh, did you see that hit! The
                     Champ's dazed. Look at his
                     face!

ANNOUNCER 2:   And DOWN he goes!

ANNOUNCER 1:   He's not getting up from that
                     one.

<u>DING! DING! DING!</u>

ANNOUNCER 2:   There it is. The ref has
                     called it! Your winner,

	Jessie "The Cannon" Tesori!
ANNOUNCER 1:	UN-BE-lievable!

THE SOUND OF THE CROWD
FADES.

SCENE 2

A LOCKER SQUEAKS AND
SHUTS.

HE PUNCHES THE LOCKER.

LOCKER ROOM DOOR SWINGS
OPEN.

MIKEY FOOTSTEPS AS HE
ENTERS.

MIKEY:	Alright. Let's see the damage.
PETE:	(VERY BOTHERED) Just go on, will ya.
MIKEY:	Busted lip. That'll be swollen tomorrow for sure. Probably gonna have you talkin' funny for a few days. We'll get some ice on it. Hematoma around your left eye. You got clocked pretty damn good.
PETE:	Jesus, Mikey. You come in here to rub it in?
MIKEY:	Come on. No fighter can go undefeated forever.
PETE:	Are you kidding me? A bleeding loss on my record to that lightweight Tesori.
MIKEY:	Jessie "The Cannon" Tesori is one of the best.
PETE:	Not even in my league, Mikey!

MIKEY:

Take it easy. This was only an exhibition match. Just a little something they felt the fans would get a kick out of. Think of it like a scrimmage. You still have your title.

PETE:

This'll be the fight everyone remembers. It doesn't matter if it's official.

MIKEY:

What do you want me to say, huh? Want me to sit here and cry about it with ya? Hold your hand for a little while? Wipe away your tears and join you for a verbal rampage on Tesori?

PETE:

Just tell me this is a dream. Tell me I'm gonna wake up in that ring again ready to fight.

MIKEY:

Yeah, maybe that's it. Maybe you're just having a little dream right now in the ring. Either way, it still means you got knocked the fuck out.

PETE:

I can't show my face in this circuit anymore. I've never lost a match and that little shit gets my number with a couple of lucky punches.

MIKEY:

You sound like a bratty child. You wanna quit and move back home to mommy in Bristol just cause you lost one fight? You're the heavyweight champ. You can't quit.

PETE:

They're gonna be showing that knock out on every channel

for the next year. I know it.

MIKEY: No matter. It's already all over the internet, kid.

PETE: What? The match just ended... (BURST OF RAGE) Cor Blimey!

> HE PUNCHES THE LOCKER SEVERAL TIMES AS HE FLIPS OUT.

Fuck technology! Fuck computers and fuck all these assholes with their stupid little smart phones! It should be illegal to put that shit on the internet.

MIKEY: Listen to yourself.

PETE: I want them arrested, Mikey. All of 'em. Lock 'em all up at Her Majesty's pleasure.

MIKEY: Come on, Butcher! Get your head straight, will ya. You're up against Sanchez after the New Year and I don't need you psyching yourself out with this one lousy defeat.

PETE: Sanchez. God damn it. That bloke is gonna throw this in my face every chance he gets. I know it. He'll be dishing out insults in every interview. Gonna do his best to embarrass me. I'll never be able to live this down.

MIKEY: No. You won't. And maybe its time for me to retire cause you threw everything I taught you straight out the window tonight.

PETE: You don't mean that.

MIKEY:	The hell I don't. I could see it all over your face. You thought this was gonna be a gimme match against Tesori and you got too cocky out there, kid. You were leaving yourself wide open. What do I always tell ya, huh? Hands up, elbows in. Every time, Butcher. It was bad form all around. You left your face wide open and your feet... they were all over the damn place. It looked like you were dancin' on hot coals.
PETE:	It felt like I had control the first round.
MIKEY:	Your feelings don't make it fact.
PETE:	I did get some solid hits in.
MIKEY:	You call those hits? I've seen kittens do more damage to a ball of yarn. Do you even remember anything from the second round?
PETE:	Yeah.
MIKEY:	Yeah? All sixteen seconds of it?
PETE:	Right outta the gate that rabid slag launched at me.
MIKEY:	Yeah, like a cannon. Blasted ya with the one-two.
PETE:	This is a career ender. It is, Mikey. One night of hard lines and I bet half my sponsors are gonna sack me after this.
MIKEY:	Alright. Enough. Have a drink. Sleep on it. There's

nothing to do now but get over it. You're "Butcher" Pete Wilcox. The Pistol from Bristol. A legend among men. Even with this loss, no one else has a record like you. And no one has a coach like you. I like to rattle your cage a bit, but I'm through listening to you derail yourself. Call it an off night. Call it a stroke of bad luck. Call it bad karma catching up to you for snubbing that Kentucky kid's "make a wish". Call it whatever you want, but you're gonna get your ass back in that ring when the time comes.

LOCKER ROOM DOOR SWINGS OPENS.

JESSIE ENTERS.

Evenin', Jessie. I think you may have taken a wrong turn.

JESSIE: Hey Mikey B. Can I speak to Butcher for a minute?

MIKEY: Uh yeah, he's right here.

JESSIE: In private please.

MIKEY: Oh. Sure thing.

PETE: She's not supposed to be in here.

MIKEY: Calm down, kid. I'll go get you that ice pack.

FOOTSTEPS.

Nice fight, Tesori.

DOOR OPENS AND CLOSES.

PETE: So, what brings you here? To the men's locker room? I can't imagine there's anything important for us to chat about.

JESSIE: (STERN) I know what you did.

PETE: What on Earth are you on about?

JESSIE: Tell me why.

PETE: Why what?

JESSIE: How much money was in it for you to fall in the second round?

PETE: What...? You think I...?

JESSIE: Don't act brain dead with me, pal. I barely tapped you and you went wobbling like a toddler learning to walk. What was in it for you, huh?

PETE: (AN IDEA IS FORMING) You really think –

JESSIE: Cut the crap, Butcher.

PETA: (CHANGE OF TONE, AMUSED, HE PLAYS ALONG, MAYBE EVEN A BRIEF CHUCKLE BEFORE SPEAKING) Well, you know I would have destroyed you if I'd gone full force.

JESSIE: That's bullshit. Are you just saying that because I'm a girl?

PETE: You have less experience. Your winning streak has been against less than formidable opponents. And yeah. You're a girl.

JESSIE: I'm not going to accept a win

	that's handed over this way.
PETE:	Take it and clear off.
JESSIE:	I would've won that match with or without you taking a dive.
PETE:	In your dreams, love.
JESSIE:	I want a rematch.
PETE:	A what? Come on. You won. Victory is yours. Congratulations on defeating "Butcher" Pete Wilcox. You'll be a legend by tomorrow morning. Someone may even write a song about ya.
JESSIE:	I called you out for a legit challenge and you've turned it into some petty game.
PETE:	My six-year-old ankle-bitin' nephew called me out last week. And guess what? I let him win too.
JESSIE:	Alright, hotshot. Next time, I'm gonna tell the conference to make it official. No more of this showcase exhibition bullshit. I bet you'd take it more seriously then.
PETE:	That'll never happen. This was a one-off event. Just something to entertain the fans.
JESSIE:	I promise you I'll make it happen. I train ten times harder than you and no one comes close to my stats in my division.
PETE:	Right. Your division. The lady's division. It doesn't

matter how much you fancy my title, you don't have a chance. They won't allow it.

JESSIE: (ANGRY) Quit being a little bitch!

PETE: Excuse me?

JESSIE: You heard me. Put on your big boy pants and bring me a real fight. I'll murder you.

PETE: You gonna bring out the "cannon", love? Is that the right or the left? I couldn't tell. They both felt like sweet kisses from your mum.

JESSIE FRUSTRATED, HITS THE LOCKER.

JESSIE: Go screw a goat, you fuckin' Irish prick.

PETE: I'm British.

JESSIE: Whatever.

PETE: (EASING THE TENSION) Settle down, will ya. I'm only taking the piss outta ya. Just having a bit of fun, that's all. Look, you connected some good shots. Gave a nice right knuckle to my jaw here. Eye is feeling a bit numb as well. And no doubt you're definitely faster than most opponents I've faced. You were striking like a bloody rattlesnake out there. You got a lotta bottle, sure, but you're far from perfect. You got flaws just like the rest of 'em. If you ever want to swing by my gym and join a session with me and Mikey B., you got an open invitation.

JESSIE: Is it the building with the sign out front that says "Chauvinistic Dickhead Training Camp"?

PETE: I invite you to get some pointers from a World Class trainer like Mikey B., and you go and say something like that?

JESSIE: Your hubris becomes you.

PETE: Listen. A lady has no place in the ring against a man. Period. I know you don't want to hear it, but that's the blunt truth of the matter. We're built differently. And that's just how things are. Oh, but we're living in this feminism generation where the female is this symbol of strength and power. So, yeah, I decided to give the World a little taste of entertainment. You know that's all they really wanted, right? The underdog victory. The iconic courageous woman overcoming the testosterone driven male. Samantha beating Goliath. And just like that the sport gets a bump in ratings. And you gain the respect of new fans that'll be at your next match, pulling for you and all your glory. Don't let 'em down is the only advice I have for you.

JESSIE: And what about you? What

	respect do you gain from this?
PETE:	One loss in an exhibition match ain't gonna break me, love. I've already shown my worth over the years.
JESSIE:	I don't know why you consider that to be honorable. You think you're doing some kinda good for women by letting me win? I don't want your charity. I want you back in that ring and I'm gonna give 'em all an honest knock out, you sorry sonuvabitch.
	DOOR OPENS AND CLOSES. MIKEY ENTERS CARRYING ICE PACK.
MIKEY:	Woah. Settle down. The match is over.
JESSIE:	I'm meeting with Jimmy first thing tomorrow. I'm gonna petition for a rematch, and if there's anyone that will be able to make it official, it's Jimmy. Don't think you've seen the last of me in the ring.
MIKEY:	Rematch? You already won.
JESSIE:	Did I?
	FOOTSTEPS. DOOR OPENS AND SLAMS AS JESSIE EXITS.
MIKEY:	Butcher, what was that all about? What'd you say to her?
PETE:	Holy shit, Mikey! She thinks I threw the fight.
MIKEY:	Threw the fight?

PETE:	Yeah. She says the punch that ended the match was barely a jab.

MIKEY:	Butcher, come on. Tell me you didn't take a dive.

PETE:	Jesus Christ, Mikey, you know me better than that.

MIKEY:	Well, I'm going to set all this straight. We don't want her damaging your credibility by spreading rumors about you faking the knockout. That would be a P-R nightmare. Let me make a few calls.

PETE:	Wellll... hold on a sec. I don't know. Maybe that's the kinda thing I need.

MIKEY:	Have you lost your mind? You want those kinds of rumors floating around about you?

PETE:	Think about it. Rumors are neutral. It's all about the perception of the audience. Rumors can be more exciting than the truth. If we let something like this get out, then people may think I was doing her a favor. Ya know? Just helping her out with her career. My title wasn't on the line, so in their eyes, they'll see that I had nothing to lose. They'll say, "Oh, there's Butcher, giving that little lady his full support. We all know he could annihilate her if he was really giving her a go." And then it's all Chinese whispers from there.

MIKEY: You want people to think that you threw the fight?

PETE: Well, here's the thing. If I ever get asked about it directly, I just tell the complete truth. I gave it my all – one hundred per cent. I'll talk about how great of a fighter she is and that sorta thing and then Bob's your uncle! They'll eat it up, Mikey. And rumors have power. Sure, many will accept the truth, but in the back of their minds there will always be some doubt. And no matter what I say...

MIKEY: They'll always wonder if you faked the knockout to make her look good.

PETE: I'll be a walking conspiracy theory!

MIKEY: I don't know, Butcher...

PETE: Come on. It's brilliant.

MIKEY: Well, at least you're not moping around anymore. And what about this rematch? What did she mean she wants to make it official?

PETE: She wants to be the champ. Who doesn't? But surely they'll never cross the men and women's division. Not for a valid title match anyway.

MIKEY: I've seen crazier things happen in my day. What if they allow it? You gonna give her a go again?

PETE: Fuck no. That girl has pit

	bulls for hands. Look at me. I haven't been this bruised up since that time I went five rounds with Ol' Tommy Colechin.
MIKEY:	Pit bulls, huh? I thought you called them lucky punches.
PETE:	Well, in the end, luck is always to blame, isn't it?
MIKEY:	You are a piece a work, you know that?

<u>GIVES PETE THE ICE PACK.</u>

Here. Get some ice on that lip. I'll tell them to pull the car around.

<u>FOOTSTEPS.</u>

<u>DOOR OPENS AND CLOSES.</u>

<u>MUSIC CUE: "BIONIC GAMES"</u>

PETE: (AMUSED, PROUD OF HIMSELF) "Butcher Pete, the Walking Conspiracy". (LAUGHS TO HIMSELF) That's good stuff.

<u>END OF PLAY</u>

JONATHAN COOK
(Host, Producer, Writer of
"Kingdumb" & "Butcher Pete")

Jonathan Cook is the creator, producer, and host of Gather by the Ghost Light. He has been involved with theatre productions for over thirty years as a playwright, director, and actor. Many of his stage plays have been produced in theaters around the world and, most recently, his full-length play Lobster Man had its world premiere at the USC Aiken Etherredge Center. He is also a seven-time recipient of the Porter Fleming Literary Award. Aside from theater work, he is also an award-winning filmmaker and, most notably, his film "Don't You Dare" was picked up for distribution on the Shorts TV Network (jonathanrcook.com)

JOHN MINIGAN
("A Monogamy of Swans")

John Minigan is a recent MA Cultural Council Artist Fellow in Dramatic Writing. Tall Tales from Blackburn Tavern, commissioned by Gloucester Stage Company, premiered in 2023. His solo adaptation of The Legend of Sleepy Hollow premiered at Greater Boston Stage Company in 2022, won the BroadwayWorld Best New Play Award, and was an Elliot Norton Outstanding New Script nominee. "Queen of Sad Mischance" won the Judith Royer Award from The Kennedy Center/-ATHE, and Noir Hamlet was an EDGE Media Best of Boston Theater awardee. John teaches at Emerson College and serves as Dramatists Guild Ambassador for the Boston region. (johnminigan.com)

STEVEN HAYET

("Hugo Saves Christmas…in May!")
Steven Hayet is a New Jersey playwright whose work has been performed from Los Angeles to London and New York to New Zealand. He is a Playwright-in-Residence at Roaring Epiphany Production Company, an inclusion theatre company providing opportunities for actors with disabilities. Selected plays include Everlasting Chocolate Therapy, Hugo Saves Christmas…in May!, Twelve Hangry Jurors, Date with Death, Playing With Fired, and Keep the Music Going. He is a proud graduate of the College of William & Mary and Rutgers University and a member of the Dramatists Guild. (stevenhayet.com)

JOHN MABEY

("Playing with Dolls &
A Tragedy of Owls")
John Mabey is a writer and storyteller whose plays have been produced in 8 countries and throughout the USA. Their multi-award winning play 'A Complicated Hope' is now published with Dramatic Publishing. Their work as a playwright is connected to their career in Psychology and their certification as a Mental Health Counselor, infusing everything they've learned about behavior, emotion and relationships into their plays. John is a published author on the topics of sexual identity and spirituality in academic books and journals. When not writing, they enjoy teaching and performing improvised comedy and true storytelling around the world. (mabeyplays.com)

SCOTT C. SICKLES
("Wheel of Fortune Reversed")
Scott C. Sickles (he/him) is an LGBTQ+ / neurodivergent / Mixed Korean American writer whose plays have been performed across the U.S., and internationally in Canada, Australia, Europe, and Asia.

Full-lengths: Nonsense and Beauty, Playing on the Periphery, Marianas Trench, and Pangea.

Published with Next Stage Press: Nonsense and Beauty, Composure, Hairdresser on Fire, From the Top, Moonlight & Love Songs, Hellish Delights, Intellectuals.

Emmy and Writers Guild of America Award winner for General Hospital.

EMILY MCCLAIN
("Tooth or Dare")
Emily McClain is an award-winning playwright, theatre maker, and educator, as well as a proud member of the Dramatists Guild. Born in Oxford, Mississippi, she now resides in Atlanta, Georgia, where she teaches theatre at the School of the Arts @ Central Gwinnett.

She is an education associate with Essential Theatre and spearheads their playwriting courses. She was named Arts ATL "Ones to Watch" for 2024 and will be one of the playwrights-in-residence with Theatrical Outfit through their "Made in Atlanta" program. Several of her plays are published through Next Stage Press.

JOHN P. BRAY
("The Demon Lady")
John P. Bray has been a Semifinalist for the O'Neill National Playwrights Conference, Semifinalist for the Princess Grace Foundation Playwrights Award, Semifinalist for the Ashland New Play Festival, Finalist for the Kernodle Playwriting Award, and Winner of the Appalachian Festival of Plays and Playwrights. His plays have had productions around the U.S. and have been published with Next Stage Press, Original Works Publishing, and in anthologies and journals.

Bray is also a screenwriter, anthology editor, and scholar. He has an MFA in Playwriting from The New School and a PhD in Theatre Studies from LSU. John teaches at UGA.

STRATON RUSHING
("Ain't the Biggest City")
Straton Rushing is a DFW-based playwright and theatremaker originally from Sonora, Texas. His playwriting honors include the Bela Kiralyfalvi Playwriting Award, the Hear Me Out Monologues Golden Ear Award, Chameleon Theatre Circle's New Play Award, Runner-Up for the McNerney Playwriting Prize and finalist for the ATHE Judith Royer Award. He holds degrees in Theatre and Philosophy from the UT Arlington and he received his MFA in Dramatic Writing from Arizona State University where he was recognized as an Outstanding Graduate for Excellence and Innovation in Creative Practice. He currently works as Administrative Coordinator for Kitchen Dog Theater. (StratonThePlaywright.com)

AVA LOVE HANNA
("Secondhand Soul")

Ava Love Hanna is a professional comedy writer, published playwright, and an award-winning speaker and storyteller. She is continually amazed by how often she is mistaken for a real grown-up. When she isn't writing plays, you can find her moonlighting as the Producing Artistic Director and podcast co-host of storiesfound.com.

RON BURCH
("Santa the Clause")

Ron Burch's plays have been produced in the USA and abroad and published in The Best Ten-Minute Plays from

GREG MANDRYK
("Unknown Number")

Greg Mandryk is a playwright residing in Cleveland, Ohio. He is a regular contributor to Cleveland Public Theatre's Dark Room and his short plays have been produced throughout the United States.

Smith & Kraus, The Best of Playground Los Angeles, and Routledge's One Minute Plays: A Practical Guide to Tiny Theatre. His films include Ferdinand (2017), for which he won the Humanitas Prize; Yours, Mine & Ours (2005); and others. He was an Executive Producer of Dinotrux and has written for Marvel Superhero Adventures, Hot Wheels City, Pretzel and the Puppies, and many others. His latest novel is JDP. (ronburch.com)

PATRICK GABRIDGE
("Santa Doesn't Live Here Anymore")
Patrick Gabridge is the producing artistic director of Plays in Place, a company that creates site-specific plays in partnership with museums and historic sites, including Mount Auburn Cemetery, the Massachusetts State House, and Boston's Old North Church. He is an award-winning playwright and has written 22 historical plays, along with many contemporary plays that have received more than 1,000 productions from theatres and schools around the world (16 countries so far). He also writes screenplays, novels and audio plays. His collection of short Christmas Comedies is entitled: Assorted Holiday Nuts. (gabridge.com)

DAVID MACGREGOR
("Immersion Therapy")
David is a playwright and screenwriter. He is a resident artist at The Purple Rose Theatre, where ten of his plays have been produced, and his work has been published by Applause, Playscripts, and Theatrical Rights Worldwide (TRW). He is the author of three Sherlock Holmes plays, all of which have been adapted into novels, and he is also the author of the two-volume nonfiction Sherlock Holmes: The Hero with a Thousand Faces. He adapted his dark comedy, Vino Veritas, into a film starring Carrie Preston, Emmy-winner for The Good Wife and star of CBS' Elsbeth. (david-macgregor.com)

JENNY LYN BADER
("Communal Table")

Jenny Lyn Bader is a playwright living in New York City. Her plays include Mrs. Stern Wanders the Prussian State Library, In Flight, and None of the Above. Her audio works include Tree Confessions (This is Not a Theatre Company) and The International Local (Subway Plays app). Her playwriting honors include the Edith Oliver Award, Athena Fellowship, and "Best Documentary One Woman Show" Award (Uni-ted Solo Fest). Her work has been published by Dramatists Play Service, Next Stage Press, Applause, Smith & Kraus, Vintage, The Lincoln Center Theater Review, Plays International & Europe, and The New York Times.
(jennylynbader.com)

DANIEL PRILLAMAN
("For a Limited Time Only")

Daniel (he/they) is a neurodivergent writer/actor/ginger currently based out of Northern Ohio. He has a special fondness for absurdism, folklore, and horror, but ultimately loves plays about honest people (or talking animals) in situations he hasn't seen before.

His full-length plays include altitude, Bereavement Leave, and Pit, a part of the '24-25 season of the Inkwell Theater's Development LAB.

Their cosmic horror, In the Slush, was a Finalist for the 2023 Princess Grace Award and is published with Ghost Light Publications.

Daniel is an alumnus of the University of Virginia and a proud member of the Dramatists Guild.

RESOURCES

[1] Gather by the Ghost Light
www.gatherbytheghostlight.com

[2] Broadway Podcast Network
https://broadwaypodcastnetwork.com/

[3] Ghost Light Publications
https://ghostlightpubs.com/

[4] Funky Little Theatre Company (Colorado Springs, CO)
https://www.funkylittletheater.org/

[5] Roaring Epiphany Production Company (Brooklyn, NY)
https://www.roaringepiphany.org/

[6] Over Our Head Players (Racine, WI)
https://overourheadplayers.org/

[7] Gardner Webb University (Boiling Springs, NC)
https://gardner-webb.edu/

[8] Hyde Park Theatre (Austin, TX)
https://www.hydeparktheatre.org/

[9] Le Chat Noir (Augusta, GA)
http://www.lcnaugusta.com/

[10] Playground LA (Los Angeles, CA)
https://playground-la.org/

[11] Phoenix Theatre Cultural Center (Indianapolis, IN)
https://www.phoenixtheatre.org/

[12] Tipping Point Theatre (Northville, MI)
https://www.tippingpointtheatre.com/

[13] The Ritz Theatre Company (Haddon Township, NJ)
https://ritztheatreco.org/

[14] Urban Stages (New York City)
https://www.urbanstages.org/

[15] Minnesota Fringe Festival
https://minnesotafringe.org/

[16] Blank Canvas Theatre (Lakewood, OH)
http://www.blankcanvastheatre.com/

ghostlightpubs.com